The Other Side of Luck

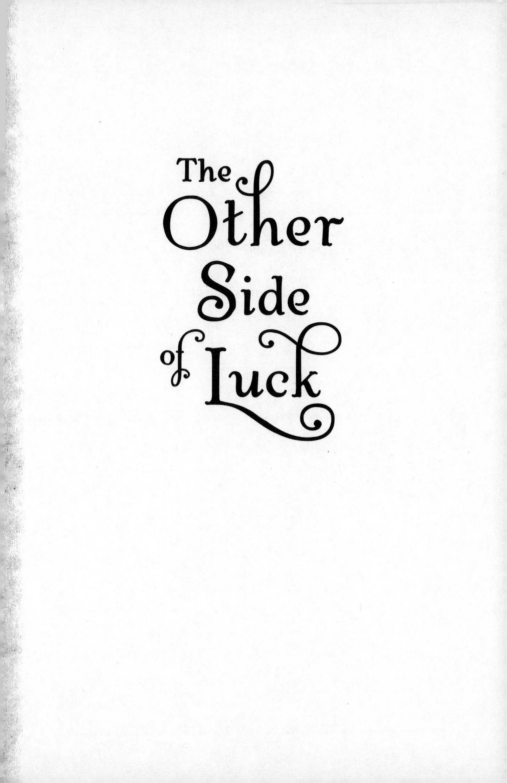

Also by Ginger Johnson

The Splintered Light

The Other Side of Luck

GINGER JOHNSON

BLOOMSBURY
CHILDREN'S BOOKS
NEW YORK LONDON OXFORD NEW DELHI SYDNEY

BLOOMSBURY CHILDREN'S BOOKS
Bloomsbury Publishing Inc., part of Bloomsbury Publishing Plc
1385 Broadway, New York, NY 10018

BLOOMSBURY, BLOOMSBURY CHILDREN'S BOOKS, and the Diana logo
are trademarks of Bloomsbury Publishing Plc

First published in the United States of America in July 2021
by Bloomsbury Children's Books

Text copyright © 2021 by Ginger Johnson
Illustrations copyright © 2021 by Lucy Rose

Bloomsbury books may be purchased for business or promotional use.
For information on bulk purchases please contact Macmillan Corporate and
Premium Sales Department at specialmarkets@macmillan.com

Library of Congress Cataloging-in-Publication Data
Names: Johnson, Ginger.
Title: The other side of luck / by Ginger Johnson.
Description: New York : Bloomsbury Children's Books, 2021.
Summary: Ignored because she is a girl, First Daughter Una sets out to find the silva flower, and
her path crosses with Julien, a pauper hoping to free his father by finding the same flower.
Identifiers: LCCN 2020054298 (print) | LCCN 2020054299 (e-book)
ISBN 978-1-68119-655-8 (hardcover) • ISBN 978-1-68119-656-5 (e-book)
Subjects: CYAC: Fantasy.
Classification: LCC PZ7.1.J615 Oth 2021 (print) | LCC PZ7.1.J615 (e-book) |
DDC [Fic]—dc23
LC record available at https://lccn.loc.gov/2020054298

Book design by Jeanette Levy
Typeset by Westchester Publishing Services
Printed and bound in the U.S.A. by Berryville Graphics Inc., Berryville, Virginia
2 4 6 8 10 9 7 5 3 1

To find out more about our authors and books visit
www.bloomsbury.com and sign up for our newsletters.

To mother and son,
the helper and the helped

The Other Side of Luck

For they too are gatherers of fruit and frankincense,
and that which they bring, though fashioned of dreams,
is raiment and food for your soul.

—Kahlil Gibran

1

Julien

In a small stone dwelling on the edge of the city Antiquitilla, a child waited to be born. The child who would become Julien knew the rhythm of his mother's heartbeat, the music of her blood flowing through her veins. He knew the trod of her footsteps and the creaking of her chair as she sat down. He knew the muted music of her voice. It was the tune he heard while floating, enfolded within her.

But on this particular spring morning, the sounds changed. Her heartbeat sped up, her footsteps slowed down, there were cries of pain, and the steady hum of his existence was traded for a shockingly loud sound. When Julien recognized that the sound came from him, he grew quiet and still, searching for his mother's heartbeat.

From above, he heard the low whine of the wind whistling through the cracks in the doorway.

From below came the sound of a beetle scuttling across the floor.

From left and right came the steady vibration of life, an unrelenting swirl of sound: a tree stretching upward, a sparrow settling into her nest, a flower bursting into bloom.

None of it was the familiar and comforting sound of his mother. Her hum had faded into silence, leaving a void that the small infant Julien did not understand.

Into that void, Julien heard another heartbeat, one similar to his mother's, but larger, if a sound could be larger. That heartbeat came with a pair of broad, steady hands that scooped up Julien and held him close.

This gentle touch should have been comforting, but another sound emerged from this person with the large hands, a sound that was jagged and fragmented. The sound settled into Julien's heart, sensitive and new. It was too much to bear alone for either of them, and so little Julien began to cry with him, his voice ragged and uncertain, but growing in intensity. The two grieved, their broken hearts knit together by sorrow.

2

Una

In the center of the city of Antiquitilla, at the Official Residence of the Magister Populi, another child—a girl—was born in a more efficient birth and to grander circumstances. On Una's first day of life, she inhaled 85,324 breaths. And in each of those breaths, she drew in a new scent: the sunlight dancing on leaves, the water tinkling in the fountain, the blood pumping through her heart. She could smell an excitement surrounding her, though she didn't understand what it meant, not yet knowing she was the first child of the Magister Populi.

On that day, one scent rose above all the others that flickered around her. It was a scent that blanketed her with feathered softness. It was a scent of sanctuary, a scent of the divine, like an archangel had just flown by. It was the scent of her mother's love, and it held her attention until her father, the Magister Populi, came to see her. His laughter rose from deep inside as he studied her face, her little toes, and her tiny fingers curling and uncurling. Although Una wished she could control her fingers, the smell of her father's laughter was almost as delicious as that of her mother's love, and she was delighted by it.

It was, however, the holy scent of her mother's love that accompanied her as she learned to sit, then stand, then walk. This was the steady scent that traveled with her as she grew, explored the gardens, went to her lessons, and wandered through the hallways and courtyards of the Official Residence.

When six years had passed, Una noticed that her mother's scent shifted slightly. It was a subtle change, as if the archangels flew a little lower. And indeed, her mother's panels of silk seemed to grow more voluminous than they already were, and her belly gradually pushed outward. Una didn't understand what this meant. She only knew that there was no room for her to sit on her mother's lap anymore.

Days before Una turned seven, her mother said to her, "Dear one, tomorrow I will go to the birthing room, and a baby will join us. You will always be my dear one, though."

"You will come back?" Una had said, placing her hands on her mother's belly, her brown skin a contrast to the pink silk.

"Yes, dear one. I will come back."

But she didn't come back. Not all day. Not the next day or the next. Una asked Ovid, the old man who served her mother, when she would return. "Your mother won't be coming back," he had said.

"Why not?"

"She is gone, child," he said in a soft voice, and he pulled her into his arms where his familiar smell surrounded her like a covering of warm syrup.

All that her mother left behind was a squalling baby boy who was whisked off to the nursery to be coddled and raised as the next Magister Populi, far from his older sister.

3

Julien

As Julien grew, he learned that his father was a collector of things for the makers in the market. Leaves, flowers, berries, bark, sap: all sorts of botanicals that could be brewed together or distilled or extracted to make balms, drinks, potions, liniments, and different kinds of refreshment.

Julien always accompanied Baba on his foraging trips, listening to the plants that grew all around. The sounds each made were delightful to Julien, the singing of sprouts and seedlings stretching and swelling, the hymn of flowers unfurling, the fusion of trees and grasses as they harmonized in their upward reach.

But Julien's favorite sounds were the steady beat of Baba's heart, the constant stretch of his muscles, and the inhale and exhale of his breath. These sounds centered him as he followed in his father's footsteps, his small legs attempting to keep up with

Baba's larger strides. As he walked behind Baba, he mirrored his every move. When Baba dodged a low-hanging branch, he dodged a low-hanging branch. When Baba avoided a puddle on the pathway, he avoided a puddle on the pathway. When Baba clambered up a large boulder, Julien clambered up the boulder.

So when Baba would lift a leaf to his nose and inhale deeply, Julien would, too.

Even if he didn't really understand why.

"Doesn't that smell wonderful?" Baba would always ask.

Julien would inhale, but he didn't know what Baba meant by smell. With the leaves at his nose, Julien could hear the chirrupy sound of the small round leaves, the deep rustle of the long broad leaves, and the whispery whistle of the narrow leaves like thin grasses. He couldn't tell their differences from his nose, though. He heard them in his heart, instead. But Baba always lifted the leaves to his nose, and Julien began to wonder if he was missing something.

In this peculiar way, Julien learned to identify plants, some by sight, but mostly by sound: the *twang* of a twig, the babble of seeds, the shrillness of stalks. He spent his days in the wilderness with Baba digging for roots, cutting small gashes into resinous bark or catching airborne seeds in a tightly woven net while the sounds of the plants frolicked around him. They even spent a few nights in the wilderness, too, in order to bring the freshest blossoms to market the next morning. Those nights were filled with a quiet, steady lullaby sung by the deep-down roots of ancient trees.

No lullabies swelled through the air on the last night they spent in the wilderness, though. That afternoon, as they were gathering elecampane, a dense fog blew in, creeping up the mountain, and it was as if a giant hand had clamped down upon all the sounds. The fog had snaked its way toward them, and when Baba had finally seen it, he picked up Julien and ran. But the legs of a man held no competition for the force of fog, and Julien and Baba had been quickly overtaken. One minute the air was clear in front of them, and the next they were enclosed in a cloud. Julien had never been so frightened in his short life.

When the cloud burst, battering them with stinging raindrops, Baba had tried to shield Julien from the weather. The roar of the rain drowned out any chirrups, rustles, and whistles from the plants, and even the steady beat of Baba's heart. It pelted down so hard and fast that Julien couldn't make out where one sound ended and another began.

Baba had run to a stand of sycamore trees and found shelter in an ancient, hollow trunk. They waited there for a very long time hoping the rain would let up, but as the afternoon passed and the darkness of night settled around them, Julien finally nodded off to sleep. When he woke the following morning, the rain had stopped, but Baba was shivering. The dampness had seeped into his lungs. Baba tried to hide the coughing, but Julien noticed that the rattle in Baba's lungs was no longer the same smooth in-and-out breath that it used to be.

As time passed, he noticed that all of Baba's sounds were creaky and rough, and the change scared him. Young as Julien was, there seemed to be very little he could do to make Baba well again, no matter how much he wanted to.

Days before Julien turned seven, Baba gave him his own collecting bag and told him that he could gather some of the leaves and flowers on his own. Though he didn't know it at the time, Baba truly needed his help. He told Julien he could hunt anywhere except the bog, for the bog was so dangerous that even Baba wouldn't set foot in it.

Julien went about his collecting with great effort, listening for the most pristine specimens, the plumpest tears of resin, the ripest fruit, and the heaviest roots, hoping his industry would make the worsening roughness in Baba's lungs go away somehow.

Baba would marvel at the quality of the resin and roots and blossoms he would bring. "How do you find them?"

Julien always shrugged. How could he tell Baba that the plants practically called to him? That he heard the push and pull of the water through their stems and leaves? It would have been as impossible for him to express as it was for him to understand what Baba meant by smell.

"I just find them," he would say. Then they would stop at the market, sell what Julien had collected, and buy some bread, usually the flat, lumpy, burned loaves that hadn't sold. Back at home, Julien would rekindle the fire if the night was cold, heat some water, and break the bread into pieces, crumbling it into the pot until he made a warm, if not particularly nourishing, supper.

And so his days went. As Julien grew bigger and stronger, Baba grew paler and weaker.

4

Una

The Magister Populi's house contained vast halls, great galleries, tinkling fountains. There were courtyards and pavilions with decorative tiles and mosaics. It had always been a place of delight to those who lived there, but now—without Una's mother—it felt like a gilded shell.

In the center of that shell were Una and her father and a small squalling infant. Una wanted it to protect the three of them while they found their way through their sorrow. She wanted to turn to her father and smell some kind of comfort from him. She wanted to meet her new brother, breathe him in, and see if she could recognize a bit of her mother in his baby scent. She wanted to be able to cling together in this shell until they could navigate their world that had so unexpectedly and tragically shifted.

But her father locked himself in his rooms. No longer were

there quick visits from him in between meetings, or games of strategy played together in the evenings. There was nothing but a closed door. Her brother's small army of caregivers repeatedly shut her out when she went to the nursery to see him. They always said he was sleeping or eating or having his diaper changed. And then *click*, they would close the door. She gave up visiting the nursery because it was clear she was not wanted.

Una was left on her own. Her only sources of comfort were the life-size portraits of her mother hanging on the cool stone walls of the corridor outside her parents' rooms. Una would sit, day after day, studying her mother's face in the paintings. One was the solemn face of a young woman at her engagement and another was the optimistic face of a new bride. The third was her favorite, though. It showed her mother holding her, a swaddled infant Una. These were faces of the past, though, and Una yearned for the face of *now*, the scent of *now*, the love of *now*. But there was no *now* with her mother. There was only *then*. She wanted her mother, but if she couldn't have her, Una needed her father to fill some of the gap left behind. She needed her brother so that she could tell him about their mother.

But she got neither.

When the door finally opened one morning and her father came out of his rooms, she was hopeful that some of their former special time together might return. But that was not to be. His eyes were hollow, his dark skin shadowed, and his face unshaven. He saw the portraits of her mother, and without a word—without even removing his hand from the doorknob—he returned to his rooms.

The next morning, the portraits were gone. In their place hung three small baskets filled with flowers. Ovid told her the portraits were too much for her father's grief, so he had them removed. Una had no say in the matter.

A year went by in this way of lifeless living. Una took to wandering the halls her mother had walked daily, seeking her scent. She also sought out her brother, visiting the nursery wing weekly. She often heard his cries and sometimes his giggles behind the door, but each time she tried to see him, she was turned away.

Two years crawled by. She rarely saw her father, as he only emerged from his grief to attend to matters of state. She rarely saw anyone, only Ovid and her tutors. Breakfast, lunch, and dinner. Spelling, literature, history. It was lonely, but the air still held whiffs of the scent of her mother's love, like the ghost of archangels, and she tried to hold on to that.

Three years passed, and Una was certain this cloud of grief would never lift. The scent of her mother was beginning to wane. As the days dragged on, Una knew that her wish of finding comfort with her father and her brother would never come to pass. It seemed as if they were no longer a family, rather three strangers living in the Official Residence. She might never inhale the delicious scent of her father's laughter again, as he buried himself in the work of governing his empire.

And her brother? Just that morning, she had heard a

conversation between his nurse and new governess through the nursery door. The nurse proclaimed that Una must blame her brother for her mother's death, and made the governess swear an oath that for his own protection, Una was never to see the boy.

Stunned, Una returned to the hallway leading to the courtyard garden where her mother had always walked. It had never occurred to her that her brother had any responsibility in her mother's death. But once that seed was planted, it grew, sending deep roots into her soul and constricting her heart. All the affection she wanted to feel for him was replaced by an unfamiliar emotion: bitterness.

She walked the long hallway, chewing on this bitterness until she heard unfamiliar voices coming her way. Una drew back behind a large pillar, hiding so she wouldn't be seen. She didn't want to talk to anyone while such bad feelings were brewing inside her.

"That's the first thing I'll change when I become Magistrix," a young woman said, pointing to a wall mosaic behind a fountain. "A fish! It should be a more powerful creature, like a stag."

Una's mouth dropped open. *When she becomes Magistrix?* Was her father going to marry again? Was this woman going to replace her mother? The woman smelled like paste. Una closed her mouth and held her breath.

"Really, Ruana? That's the first thing?" an older woman said. "I'd get rid of the daughter before I did anything else."

Una gasped, then nearly choked at the older woman's foul breath. *Get rid of the daughter?*

The first woman opened her eyes wide. "You think she might be a problem?"

"Daughters always are." The older woman smiled, then elbowed the younger one. "Why do you think we're here, dear daughter?"

Una got a good look at the two women as they passed by. The younger one had thick hair piled atop her head in elaborate braids and twists, and wore pink and purple silks with a wide red sash. She looked like an exotic bird. The older woman, in contrast, had the look of a common crow, crafty and sly in her simple dark dress.

Una tried to forget the scent of paste and bad breath, but the smells lingered as she wondered if this could be true. If it *was* true, what would happen to her?

All kinds of possibilities went through her mind, each one worse than the last. Una ran into the courtyard garden. She tucked herself into a mossy corner behind a bushy plant with heart-shaped leaves and breathed deeply to relieve all the bitter tightness inside.

5

Una

Una stayed hidden behind the plant, drawing in its scent until all traces of the women's smells were gone. It wasn't until she heard the familiar trod of Ovid's feet that she emerged from the mossy corner.

"There you are, my little flower. I've been looking for you," Ovid said. He studied her face, then furrowed his brow. "Is something troubling you, sweet pea?"

Una nodded. "Is my father going to marry again?"

Ovid's face turned grave. "Yes, sweetling."

"Why did no one tell me?"

"Your father wanted to tell you himself."

"Well, he didn't! I thought he was still sad."

"He is, but a Magister must have a Magistrix, and it's been too long that he's gone without one. Perhaps this new wife will make him less sad."

Una thought this over. She didn't want her father to be sad, but *she* was still sad.

Ovid's mouth softened at the sight of the bush with the heart-shaped leaves. "Your mother spent much time in this garden when she was expecting you."

Una looked up at him. "She did?"

"No one loved these plants like she did, and no one has cared for them in quite the same way since she's been gone. Perhaps you would like to learn?"

"Could I?"

Ovid nodded, and with that, the mossy corner—a corner that held unfortunately neither her mother nor her mother's scent—carried the promise of something else. Something like sanctuary. And what a lucky thing that was. Though it seemed as if the last traces of her mother were about to be completely erased from the rest of the Official Residence, Una wouldn't let that happen here.

Day after day, she found refuge in the courtyard garden. Ovid taught her to clip and prune while her father's elaborate wedding plans were made. The plants never seemed to mind as she plucked off leaves and twisted branches to let their scent perfume the air. She weeded and watched and watered and waited. She guided her mother's plants into shapes, turning bushes into balls, pyramids, and cubes, and eventually into more elaborate shapes, like fish, snakes, and dragons. She always let the scent of each plant govern what she did.

Inside the Official Residence, the shimmers of her mother's

18

scent were slowly being overpowered by the smell of paste, as Ruana bustled about making arrangements for a grand ceremony. It seemed as if all the archangels that had once hovered near had vanished, making it harder and harder for Una to remember that scent of her mother's love.

Ruana would never be a mother to Una, for she was far too busy with other matters. The only time Ruana ever talked to her was when she asked if Una would like to wear a yellow dress or one of lavender? Would she like to carry a bouquet of orchids or petunias? Did she think chocolate was good for dessert or should there be fruit? Una never responded.

Once, Una caught Ruana looking at her oddly. Una got up and walked away, for she was certain that Ruana was thinking of ways to "get rid of the daughter."

When the wedding day came, Una wore a yellow dress with lavender stripes. She carried a bouquet of orchids and petunias. She ate chocolate-covered fruit for dessert. Guests murmured how lovely the day was, but Una just wanted it to be over.

She looked at Ruana sitting next to her father. She seemed tiny, bird-like, but very sure of herself. Una's father was the essence of power, all muscle and ceremonial braids, might and self-assurance that matched Ruana's own. Ruana now sat in her mother's seat, took her mother's place at the table, and would speak while her mother never would again. It made Una's mouth chalky.

At the far end of the table was a very solemn little boy with

19

a halo of black crinkly hair. He had a sweet face the same shape as her father's. Una's heart squeezed inside of her. Here was the brother she had yearned to love when he was born.

The brother who had been kept from her.

The brother who had caused her mother's death. She felt her face harden.

He glanced at Una and flinched as if he were afraid of her. Una put the chocolate-covered fruit down on her plate and left the table.

The wedding over, Ruana quickly settled into the Official Residence. Ruana's presence made her mother's absence so much more pronounced. The scent of paste lay heavy in the air and became stronger as it grew clear that a new baby was on the way. Una was soon going to have another sibling.

6

Una

Una missed her mother most at night when she couldn't sleep. During those times, she would turn to her collection of scents to help her. She kept bottles and jars filled with flower buds, essential oils, resins. Anything that carried a strong scent. But there were times when not even her collection could soothe her into slumber, so Una took to wandering the halls and the courtyards. At night with no one around, she could almost smell her mother's archangels. Almost.

Una often visited the older topiaries in her garden, the dragons flanking the gates and the sea monster in the rear. They were like old friends because they had been there for as long as she could remember. She would think about riding a dragon up, out, and away from the Official Residence, away from her stepmother, away from her father, away from the brother she didn't know. She thought about riding the sea monster through the waves to a place where the salty sea air could settle into her soul, and she could search for something to remind her of the scent of her mother. But such rides to freedom were only a fancy in her mind that left her feeling empty.

One night while walking around the courtyard and wishing for something beyond the walls of the Official Residence, Una stood at the garden window, an opening in the wall framed and divided by twists of wrought iron. Una clutched the metal bars and poked her nose into the still air. Below the window, large clusters of tiny white blossoms glowed in the moonlight. Una studied the blossoms and wondered how they came to be planted there. No other flowers grew on that side of the wall. Perhaps her mother threw seeds from the window, hoping they'd grow.

As she studied them, a large green caterpillar climbed one of the stems, causing it to sway under its weight. The enormity of the caterpillar both fascinated and repulsed her. Its rippling movement brought it ever closer to the white blossoms.

Her arm was not long enough to reach through the bars to flick the caterpillar off the plant. If she left to get a branch to reach it, the caterpillar would surely have begun feasting before she returned.

"Go away, caterpillar!"

The caterpillar halted below the collection of blooms. She

occurred to her that she wasn't the only one to receive it. She felt almost jealous.

Cassius continued, "I never got to say goodbye. I was angry that she wanted to leave to marry, and I hid so she wouldn't leave. But she left anyway."

He looked away, but Una could smell his sadness. The cloudy scent conveyed a gloom that she knew only too well.

"I suppose she had to go. The Magister Populi wouldn't—or couldn't—change his schedule to suit the whims of a six-year-old boy." Cassius paused, regret sitting heavily upon his shoulders. "I never saw her again. The journey was too long for chance visits, and I was not allowed to travel the road by myself. As the years passed, I planned to come as soon as I was old enough. I wanted to surprise Cassandra, but by the time I arrived, it was too late. She was already gone."

The two of them stood together in the quiet, their grief connecting them through the wall.

Cassius spoke into the darkness. "I have been here ever since, trying to come to terms with her death."

"Why didn't you make yourself known to my father? If he knew who you were, you would be our guest here, not one of the guards."

Cassius shook his head. "Our families have never been easy with each other. Theirs was undoubtedly an arranged political marriage. An attempt to make peace between us."

Una wasn't sure if he was joking or not, because her parents had truly loved each other. "Really?"

"Your father never told you about the history between our two families?"

"My father hasn't told me much of anything," Una said, thinking of all the time he spent in his rooms.

Cassius looked at her with a calculating eye. "Interesting."

"Will you tell me?"

"I will kindly decline," he said slowly. "Your father must have his reasons, and I will respect that. I am certain he would not be happy that I am here, especially as one of his guards. Now that I've gotten to see a bit of Cassandra in you, I will return home."

Una's heart dropped. Just as she was given an uncle, she was losing him. "But there is so much more that I want to know about my mother," she said. "And you, too. Don't go."

Cassius studied her, then said, "Why don't you come with me? You can meet your grandparents and the rest of your aunts and uncles and cousins."

Una blinked. Grandparents? Aunts and uncles and cousins? Why hadn't she realized that she might have more family? Probably because her father had no other family, having lost a sister in childhood and both parents when he was a young man. This was a stunning revelation, almost as stunning as the fact her uncle stood on the other side of her garden window. "Come with you? Could I?"

"You would be most welcome."

She would ask her father, the Magister Populi, if she could go—at least for a visit. His governing duties kept him so busy, he would never know she was gone. And she would be far from the growing smell of paste. Her wish to fly beyond the walls of the Official Residence was coming true. And she might even have the chance to find her mother's scent. Find it *and* breathe it in all the time.

"Thank you . . . Uncle." Una tried the word to see how it fit. She had never called anyone uncle before. It felt right. After all, he carried her mother's same mannerisms and expressions, perhaps even bore a bit of the scent of archangels. "I will go."

He smiled, and Una felt his grief—and her own—lift. She wasn't carrying the weight of it by herself anymore and the relief surprised her.

"I will need to make some arrangements," Cassius said.

"Of course. I will ask my father and—"

Cassius interrupted her. "It might be best if you didn't. Goodbyes are hard. That's one thing I know very well."

Una was troubled by his words. She had spent little time with her father over the past five years, but how could she leave on such a journey without at least saying goodbye? He *was* her father. "I'll think about it."

Cassius smiled. "Tomorrow? I should have all the arrangements made by then."

Una's enthusiasm faltered. "So soon?"

"My parents are growing old. They won't want to miss one more minute of your life, seeing as how they've missed, what? Twelve years?"

"Almost twelve. My birthday is next month," Una said.

Cassius nodded. "Tomorrow then."

Una watched him fade into the darkness and wondered if this was the right thing to do. There was little doubt in her mind that he was her uncle—the resemblance to her mother was too strong. But to leave without asking permission or saying goodbye? Una bit her lip, uncertain.

She hurried through the garden, then called for Ovid.

The old man appeared with a lit candle, his eyes blinking and squinting in the light. "What do you wish, First Daughter?"

"I want to know about my mother."

Ovid rubbed his eyes. "Your mother would want you to be asleep at this hour—as do I—but seeing how you are not, what do you wish to know? I will tell you if I am able."

"Did my mother have a brother?" Una asked, though she was certain she knew the answer. Cassius couldn't be lying. Even his scent seemed related to the scent of her mother, if a bit inkier.

"I do not know of your mother's family. She did not speak of her home, other than to say it was far—two months' journey."

"So she could have had a brother?"

"She could have had ten brothers for all I know. Ten brothers and ten sisters, along with a host of aunts, uncles, and cousins. What I can tell you, my night-blooming flower, is that it would be well for you to sleep now."

Una let herself be guided to her rooms and settled under the silk sheets on her bed, but she couldn't sleep. She considered taking out her scent collection, but knew instinctively that it would not be enough to settle her. So Una sat up and let the darkness of the night envelop her like a hug. Great salty tears fell from her eyes, but she wasn't sure if they sprang from what was lost or what was found.

8

Julien

When Julien was nearly twelve, Baba began testing him. The time was approaching when he would be brought before the other collectors to demonstrate his knowledge. It was a rite of passage in order to be accepted among the buyers at the market. Nerves dogged Julien about this, because although he could identify most of the common botanicals by their individual melodies, he didn't understand scent, and Baba always asked about scent.

On Baba's good days, he would join Julien on the trail, questioning him as they walked. This was a good day, and Baba began by pointing to a shrubby tree.

"This one?"

Julien listened to the steady *thump-thump* of the sap. "Terebinth!"

Baba pulled out a handful of dried leaves and lifted them to

Julien's face. This was much harder. "Inhale," he said. "Smell this. What is it?"

Julien obediently inhaled, and tried to identify the leaves the way Baba did—but inhaling didn't magnify the sound. In fact, there was only a rustle. Still, Julien listened hard for the plant's whisper.

"Artemisia?"

"Well done!"

Baba pulled out another handful of petals and coughed. He dropped the petals into Julien's hands, trying to catch his breath. Julien listened to Baba for a moment. This cough wasn't one of the bad ones. He lifted the petals to his ear, listening for the scent, but Baba's coughing covered any sound there might have been.

"Patchgrass blooms?" Julien asked.

Baba, having recovered his breath, elbowed him in the ribs. "You're joking, aren't you? It's gardia."

Julien, who had been quite serious, broke out into a big smile. "Of course. How could I mistake that for patchgrass?"

Baba laughed, but a troubled feeling rained down on Julien. He didn't understand how he could have known this. He didn't feel ready to be questioned by the other collectors, nor did he think he would be ready until he figured out this elusive smelling.

9

Una

When morning came, Una waited for Ovid to appear. At the sound of his tread upon the stone outside her door, she flew to the entry. "I need to speak to my father immediately."

Ovid stopped short, surprised at the intensity on her face. "First, you have middle-of-the-night questions about your mother and now you seek audience with your father? Whatever do you want to see him about, my sweet blossom? What can be so important that you interrupt his morning meetings?"

Una bit her lip. She wanted to tell Ovid her secret, but wasn't sure if she should. She decided against it, and simply said, "I have a question for him."

"It must be important, if you go to him uninvited."

"Yes," she said. "It is."

The walk to the cabinet room was long, and Una questioned her decision with every footfall. What if he was angry at the interruption and she lost the courage to ask him when she arrived? Or what if she asked him, and he forbid her from going? On the other hand, what if he said she could go and then asked her not to return? After all, he had a new wife and another child coming any day.

There were so many ways this could go wrong.

Una followed Ovid into the part of the Official Residence that housed the government rooms. But as she fretted about what might happen, she was slapped with the odor of paste. *Ugh.* Her stepmother must be near.

She heard heavy breathing up ahead, then a whimper. Una looked at Ovid. He frowned, and they continued on their way. The scent of paste grew stronger, and the whimper turned into a cry.

"I fear something is wrong," Ovid said, hurrying forward.

Una knew it was her stepmother. The baby must be coming. But why was she in the corridor to the government rooms? Una nearly gagged at the smell. The cries grew louder, and Una hung back. Nothing good ever came of childbirth, and even though she had no love for her stepmother, she was fearful after what had happened to her mother.

Ovid kneeled by the suffering woman and urged Una forward. "Stay with her while I get the birthing room prepared."

Una blanched at the thought, but Ovid was already hurrying down the hall. The woman before her moaned loudly and grabbed Una's hand, squeezing until her fingers went numb.

After some time, Ruana loosened her grip, but didn't let go

of Una's hand. "You won't leave me? Please, I don't want to be alone."

Una shook her head and patted Ruana's shoulder awkwardly. The motion caused a puff of paste scent to waft toward her. She had to turn away.

Ruana began to moan again, this time louder than before. She rocked back and forth and began weeping.

A door opened down the hall.

"You there!" A man stood at the doorway. "What is the meaning of this disturbance?"

Una had never been addressed in such a manner. She faced the man, but she didn't recognize him. Clearly, he didn't recognize her or the suffering Magistrix at her side, either.

At that moment, her stepmother seized Una's shoulder and a long low cry escaped her lips.

The man spoke again. "You are interrupting my business with the Magister Populi."

Una stretched herself into her proudest stance and said, "I don't care what business you have with the Magister Populi. I am the First Daughter and this is the Magistrix. You should not talk to us in that way."

The Magistrix cried out again, and the Magister Populi appeared in the doorway, resplendent in a peaked cap with a line of bright jewels along its edge. He took in the scene with one swift glance. "Una! You're hurting the Magistrix!"

"No, I'm not!"

Before anyone could say more, Ovid came rushing around

the corner with the old midwife. They made quick perfunctory bows to her father, and then they gathered the Magistrix in their arms and led her away.

Left alone, Una gave one last look at her father and the man standing in the doorway, and fled down the hallway, back to her room.

10

Una

Una paced, angry and hurt. Her father didn't ask any questions before jumping to conclusions. Well, if he assumed the worst of her, she would go. She would pack up her things and be ready to leave once Cassius had made arrangements.

She began pulling out her clothes, the ones that were the most comfortable, the ones that were the most beautiful. Then she pulled out shoes and jewelry and other trinkets that she wanted to have with her: her gardening tools, a knife, a gold bottle that was her mother's, her scent collection.

It wasn't long before she heard Ovid calling from outside her door. "Una, your father, the Magister Populi, wishes to see you."

"I don't wish to see him." She turned her face toward the wall and closed her eyes, trying to shut out the memory of his harsh words. It was true that she hadn't wanted to help her stepmother, but that was only because of the smell. Well, mostly. She certainly didn't want to *hurt* her.

Ovid knocked one last time, then opened the door. He bowed and said, "Your father awaits." The skin of his face hung, making his mouth appear to be in a perpetual frown. Una was quite certain that even if his skin were young and smooth, his mouth would be in a frown right now anyway.

With a hint of disapproval, he glanced at the things she had strewn about her room, then turned and led the way down the corridor, turn after turn, retracing their steps from earlier.

"You have not asked after the Magistrix, which I'm certain must be an oversight on your part, considering her delicate condition," he gently reprimanded her.

Una huffed. "I didn't think anything I said would make a difference."

"No, you are right, but it is the civil and kind thing to do."

"How is she, then?"

"She labors." When he reached the anteroom to the government chamber, he scanned the girl to make sure nothing was amiss in her appearance.

"Is he very angry?"

Ovid looked grave. "I would think it likely—he was negotiating with that man we saw earlier."

Una shrugged. Her father was always negotiating something.

"Negotiating for your future."

When Una didn't respond, Ovid clarified, "For your hand in marriage."

All the air left Una's body as if she had been punched. Certainly her father must see that she was far too young to be married, mustn't he?

Ovid didn't notice and kept talking. "After what happened this morning, the Magister Populi might have you married to a toothless fool who will require his crusty feet to be massaged each morning."

That was enough to jump-start Una's lungs. "He wouldn't dare."

"Let's hope." Ovid opened the door, bowing low. "Presenting Una, First Daughter of our Magister Populi."

Una curtsied deeply, head down until her father's voice released her. "Rise."

She stood, a slight cramp in her lower back, but kept her head bowed in deference. All she could see were his feet, shod in leather sandals. "You have called, Magister Populi."

"You interrupted my negotiations for your marriage."

"It wasn't I who interrupted them, Father. I was on my way to ask you a question when I came upon your wife in the midst of her labor. I was only trying to help." Una waited, but her father didn't respond immediately.

A full minute passed before he said, "I see. In other words, you would have interrupted if the Magistrix hadn't beaten you to it."

Una bit her lip. No doubt her father was a skilled negotiator. "I . . . I suppose so."

She clasped her hands together and bowed her head lower,

waiting for her father's anger. Instead, the Magister Populi roared with laughter, which she hadn't heard in years. The scent of his laughter was as delicious as it was unexpected— spicy, aromatic, and somewhat peppery. "Daughter, have no fear. That man was not one I would want as a son-in-law. Besides, you are too young. Your mother would say so, too. Now, tell me. What is it that you wished to ask me?"

The scent of his laughter washed away all of Una's anger at the earlier injustice, and suddenly, Una felt six again, wanting to be important to her father. She would tell him about Cassius and his invitation, rather than simply leaving without saying goodbye. She looked up at him, studying his features, trying to guess what he might say about Cassius.

"Actually, I wanted to talk to you about my mother."

Once again, an interruption came before she could go any further.

A servant entered the large hall, bowed to her father, and said, "The Magistrix wishes me to congratulate you on the birth of a son." Then he bowed to Una and said, "She wishes me to convey her gratitude to the First Daughter for her kindness and invite her to meet her new brother as soon as she is able."

A delighted smile came over the Magister Populi's face. Without another look at Una, he rose from his chair and followed the servant toward the door. He called over his shoulder, "We'll talk again soon, yes?"

Una nodded, but felt tears prick her eyes. Her father hadn't even glanced back at her.

11

Una

Back in her rooms, Una thought over the events of the day, from her desire to speak to her father, to her stepmother's labor, to her would-be suitor's self-importance, to her father's disregard of her in order to see the new infant.

She felt very alone. If she had been uncertain about leaving with Cassius, she was no longer. No one at the Official Residence would miss her. No one even bothered with her except for Ovid.

Una surveyed her belongings strewn across the room and bit her lip. This was a much bigger undertaking than she had thought. Uncle Cassius hadn't said anything about how much she could take. Perhaps this was too much?

She needed something to settle her nerves before she could finish packing. In front of her sat a box full of vials containing her scent collection, smells that made her calm or courageous or energized. Una needed some courage, for she did not know what the rest of the day would bring.

She opened her collection, closed her eyes, and allowed her finger to drift over the vials, moving wherever it willed. Her finger was drawn toward a vial at the back of the box. She opened her eyes to see which one she had picked.

It was one that she didn't often sample, in part because it was bitter. Its harshness always brought her to tears. By the end of her time with it, though, she always felt strong, as if she could take on the world. It was a good choice, for today she would need all the strength she could get. A long journey lay ahead of her, ending in an unknown place with unknown people.

She twisted off the cap and inhaled deeply. Harshness turned to bitterness, and the tears flowed freely down her cheeks. Despair, a sadness as old as the eternities, filled her and she questioned her choice of this vial. She always did at this stage of the smell. But once the despair lifted, there would be room for courage. It was a struggle to reach that point, though.

Yet here it came, a sharp cleanness that grew stronger with each passing second. Slowly, a feeling of invincibility came over her. She closed the cap on the vial, then returned it to its place. More powerful and clearheaded now, she slid the box into her bag, cinched it, and tucked it away.

Undoubtedly, there was too much here to bring with her. She would first pack a bag with the items she absolutely needed like her scent collection, and then pack other bags that could come with her if there was room.

Una wondered what her mother's ancestral home was like. She hoped it was as beautiful as the Official Residence. She imagined her mother at her own age, full with wishes and wants. Maybe she had her own set of rooms that Una could stay in. What a gift that would be to gain a new piece of her mother that way.

An image of her grew in Una's mind. She could see the pattern on her mother's silk. She could feel her mother's leg as she pressed against it. "Mum!" she would say. She was anxious to hear what her mother would say back. Might she speak words of love? Advice? Una waited, listening for the mother in her mind to speak. But she was silent, her face blank.

Was that what her mother's eyes really looked like? Or was that just what they looked like in the portraits she had spent so many hours studying?

Una wasn't sure, and the uncertainty weighed heavily on her. What she feared most was forgetting. If she forgot her mother's scent, she would forget her mother, and that was unthinkable.

Into these thoughts came Ovid, bearing a large tray. "The kitchens sent something to tempt you, if only there were someplace to set it down. Sweet child, has a whirlwind come through here?"

Una shifted a pile of clothes from table to bed. Ovid set down the tray and lifted the cover to show chilled melon cut into the shape of a swan. "They wanted to send some concoction they call 'The Magistrix gasped' in honor of your new brother but I talked them into something simple."

"This is simple?" Una walked around the swan inspecting the fruit sculpture, from its intricate feathers and beak to the elaborately carved flowers surrounding it.

"It is simple in comparison." He frowned.

Una stared at the swan. Its eyes dripped juice. "You have always been kind to me, Ovid."

"Your mother was the delight of my life—may she rest in peace—and you, my little bumblebee, are just like her." He smiled at Una.

Her heart cracked at the mention of her mother. She couldn't smile back. Her mother. Her mother's love. Her mother's scent. Gone. A bead of juice dripped down the bird's bill.

"Perhaps the news I bring might give you cheer, since this weeping avian does not."

Una looked up. "You have news?"

"Your father has sent out a proclamation requesting a silva flower for your twelfth birthday. He said it reminded him of your mother, and after your visit, he thought you would like one for the courtyard garden." Ovid glanced at her with a smile on his lips.

Una froze, stricken with what Ovid had said. Her mother had never liked silva flowers. That had been their secret. She thought they were too grand and showy, that their scent was cloying. But her father gave them to her every year on their anniversary. He never knew that Una's mother had them removed—with relief—at the end of the day.

"It was supposed to be a surprise, but it seemed as if you could use some cheer today. Does this not make you happy?"

Una forced her lips into a smile, feeling more alone than she had before. "How kind and generous my father is."

She looked at the melon swan with its weepy eyes. At least Una would have company in her misery. She decided she would call this particular dish "Una cried."

12

Una

When darkness settled and Una had all of her necessities packed, when Ovid disappeared into the depths of the Official Residence, when the insects stopped droning and the perfume of the flowers ascended into the still air, Una returned to the courtyard garden. She carried three bags, and a small trunk sat at her feet. She hid in a leafy corner to await the caravan Cassius had arranged. She wondered if she should have left a letter for Ovid explaining where she was going so he wouldn't worry. Clearly, no one else would care. But it was too late, for she heard Cassius's footsteps approaching.

When he reached the garden window, Una said, "Is everything ready?"

Cassius smiled. "You must be even more anxious to go than I am. Yes, I have a horse for us. She's old, but can still make the journey."

"One horse?" Una's voice rose in surprise.

"There were no others to be had."

"Oh." Una knew she led a privileged life as the Magister Populi's daughter, but she hadn't thought they would be traveling with just one horse. "Is the journey possible with only one?"

"The horse will carry our provisions, and we'll have to walk. You can't bring much, but you shouldn't need much anyway. Are you wearing boots?"

Una nodded, grateful that she had had the sense to wear boots. She had debated about wearing her prettiest dress to make a good impression on her grandparents, but then decided it might not survive the journey. Instead she packed her pretty dress in her bag of essentials and wore the plain gardening clothes—loose trousers and a tunic. She would switch to her dress when they were closer.

Una looked at the bags at her feet, knowing the rest of her pretty things would have to stay behind. She swallowed that disappointment when she thought of her mother. Leaving her bags behind was a small price to pay.

"We'll go through the rear gate near the rubbish pit," Cassius continued. "The guard is careless this time of night. He usually sleeps."

Cassius took out a ring of keys and tried one after another in a lock at the window.

"There's a lock here?" Una asked. "I never knew."

"You can only see it from outside. It's set into the wall."

Cassius found the right key and with a click, the iron bars opened.

Una hitched up her bag of essentials—her collection of vials, her gardening trowel and clippers, a knife, a pair of loose trousers, the pretty dress she would wear to meet her grandparents, the small gold bottle that had been Una's mother's, some dried pears, and a flask of cold, clear water—and passed it to Cassius. She took one last look at the garden she had so lovingly tended. She pictured Ovid, patiently showing her what to do. She loved his familiar scent of warm syrup, but she needed her mother's smell of archangels more. Her mother had come here to have her. Now she needed to go there to have her mother. Besides, no one would miss her. Not with a new baby boy to fuss over.

"Goodbye," she whispered. The journey ahead would undoubtedly be difficult, but there would be a sweet prize at the end: her mother's family. *Her* family.

13

Julien

As they approached their last stop—a tree that gave gener-
ously of its resin—Baba saw the slashes Julien had cut in its
bark. The resin had seeped out and hardened into tears.

"Well done, Julien!" Baba said. "These will fetch a nice
price! We could eat like kings tonight if they're ready!"

Julien stopped walking and listened. They would be ready
if they made a crumbly-crinkle sound. At a gloompy *slosh*, his
heart sank. "No luck, today. They're not ready yet, Baba."

"How do you know?" Baba touched one of the teardrop-
shaped drips of resin.

Julien shrugged. "They tell me if they're ready or not."

Baba looked strangely at Julien. "You are right. They're not
ready. I guess we'll eat like paupers again. Well, come then.
Let's go home. Perhaps we'll be able to find some bread at the
market."

Julien wished the tears of resin had been ready so he could buy some soup to help Baba's cough. There was always a soup-seller at the market, the tiniest old woman with the biggest pot of soup hanging over a makeshift fire. Her voice crackled and the spices in the soup pot always sang out. But there would be no soup tonight.

He followed Baba back toward the city, through the gates, past the water troughs, and west toward what remained of the market at that late hour. Many of the sellers had sold out and were gone, but there was still one lone baker with some sad and burnt-looking loaves.

The baker looked at Julien, then at Baba. "Two loaves?"

Baba pulled a coin out of his pocket and handed it to the man.

The baker peered at it, then flipped it over, weighing it in his hand. He looked back at Baba. "One."

"Two," Baba said, taking one small, misshapen loaf and holding out his hand for another. "You should know a good thing when you see it. Your bread is fit for pigs, or else you wouldn't have any left."

The baker narrowed his eyes and grudgingly handed over another loaf.

Julien hoped the bread was better than pig food, as that was all they had to eat. He would boil some water and soak it for Baba. It was a far cry from what the soup-seller had, but hopefully it would ease Baba's cough and help him to sleep.

The two headed through the maze of market stalls. As

Baba rounded a corner, he nearly ran into a man standing on a box. The man looked as if he had been there all day, repeating the same news over and over. Grateful for a new audience, he shouted:

"The Keeper of the Kept, the Great Magnifico, Overlord and Magnate, Dynastic Monarch, the Magister Populi reigns from the east sea to the west sea, one hundred twenty-three provinces. His deeds are great and his conquests many. His name strikes fear in the hearts of his enemies. Those who are loyal to him live in prosperity and peace.

"On this day, the Magister Populi sends a message to his subjects. The first person to bring him a specimen of the rare and fragile night-blooming silva in honor of his first daughter's twelfth birthday shall be greatly honored and greatly rewarded."

14

Julien

Baba coughed only once during this recitation, but Julien could see that the message awoke some kind of emotion in him. Julien had never heard of silva flowers and didn't much care about them. Unless they could bring Baba health and new life, he had other, more pressing things to think about—like getting Baba warm and fed.

At home, Julien wrapped Baba in their one blanket. It did little to quell his shivering. He was afraid Baba had done too much that day and the consequences would be long-lasting. But maybe tonight sleep would settle into his chest and bind up whatever was broken and loosen whatever was restricted. Maybe tonight sleep would heal him.

It was into these worries that Baba said, "The Magister used to request silva flowers for the first Magistrix once a year, always for their anniversary."

Julien had already forgotten about the messenger and the request for the silva flower. From his bag, he pulled a handful of dried grass, leaves, and twigs he had picked up on the way home and set it in their hearth to start a fire.

"I heard that after she died, the Magister never once asked for another silva." Baba was silent a moment, lost in his thoughts.

"Did you ever see her? The first Magistrix?" Julien drew the steel against his flint, throwing a spark into the small pile of tinder. The pile didn't ignite, so he tried again.

"See her? Oh, yes. I knew her quite well."

That startled Julien and the steel glanced off the flint. "You knew her? How? Why didn't you tell me that you knew her?"

"That was a long time ago—before you were born."

Julien struck the steel against the flint again, throwing several sparks into the dry tinder. This time, one caught hold, and he nursed the flame, feeding it with small twigs until it grew into a steady fire.

"What was she like?" Julien asked, hanging a small kettle of water above the fire.

Baba smiled. "She was a lovely woman. Aside from your mother, she was the kindest person I ever knew. When the Magistrix smiled, the whole world smiled with her. Once you knew her, you couldn't help but do your best to delight her."

"How did you meet her, Baba?"

"I came upon her enormous caravan as she journeyed to the city. I could tell she was important because of the number of people accompanying her, but I didn't know she was soon to be the Magistrix. She stopped the caravan when she saw me collecting and asked what I was doing. I told her that I was gathering angel's wings. She laughed and asked me what they were. I gave her a small bouquet of the finest ones that I had found that day. She lifted them to her nose and breathed them in. 'This,' she said, 'is like breathing in light.'"

Julien wondered what it felt like to breathe in light. He checked the water. It was beginning to steam.

Baba continued, "She never forgot a face, and when I saw her next, she asked how I was, and how my family was. I told her that I didn't have a family yet. 'Surely you must want a family?' she asked. I was too embarrassed to tell her that I hadn't enough money to support a family, but she guessed. She gave me that flint and steel. She said it was a payment for the flowers I had given her before. I didn't want to accept it, for they had been a gift, but she insisted. So I brought her more angel's wings the next time I found some. And she gave me this blanket. I brought her another bouquet, and she gave me that kettle. Every time I tried to repay her, she found a way to give me something back—something that I would need to support a family."

Julien found himself warmed by the generosity of this woman.

"Eventually, she requested that I become her chief gardener and I cultivated angel's wings for her, because she said they were quickly growing to be her favorite scent. But she really marveled when I brought her some after a frost. When it gets cold enough, the frost forms crystals along the leaves, turning them into wings—miniatures of the kind you could believe belong to archangels. She was absolutely delighted and kept bouquets of them chilled so she could enjoy the delicate ice."

"She sounds like she was a wonderful person." The water was ready, so Julien broke the hard bread into a bowl, then poured the steaming water over it, stirring to soften the bread. "What happened? Why are you no longer head gardener at the Official Residence?"

Baba smiled wistfully. "A much more important job came along."

"What could have been more important than being head gardener at the Official Residence?"

"You, my son. You."

Julien stopped stirring and looked at the softness in Baba's eyes. When his mother died, someone had to take care of him. That someone was Baba. It never occurred to him that being a father would leave no time to tend the gardens of the Magistrix.

"You gave up a lot."

"I received even more."

Once the bread softened, Julien gave the porridge a final stir, and handed the bowl and spoon to Baba.

"There is too much here," Baba said. "You must take some."

"I've already had some," Julien lied. "The bread expands. That's why it looks like more. Besides, I had some wood sorrel and cress while we were out collecting."

"I think you're lying to me," Baba said, with a shrewd look

in his eye. "But I also know you won't eat if I don't, so I'll make you a deal. I'll eat what I can, and then you eat the rest, yes?"

Julien agreed, and settled at Baba's feet. "I'm sorry you gave up being head gardener for me."

"You weren't the only reason. There was a rather nasty under-gardener who was quite ambitious. He was happy to take my place. But he never had the light touch that the angel's wings needed. I heard a blight came through and killed all of them."

Baba took a bite of the porridge.

Julien puckered his eyebrows. "I don't understand. If angel's wings were the Magistrix's favorite scent, why did the Magister give her silva flowers?"

Baba paused, the spoon halfway to his mouth. He set the spoon back into the bowl. "I've wondered that myself for many years. I think perhaps it had more to do with the Magister than the Magistrix."

"What do you mean?"

"The silva flower is very rare. It's difficult to find because it grows in wet soil—bogs, usually—and it blooms only once a year at night, although you can force it to bloom other times. Angel's wings, on the other hand, flower throughout the season, and will continue to flower until the weather changes and they freeze. I think he saw the Magistrix as a rare bloom, and he wanted to give her something as rare and as precious as he thought she was."

Julien nodded, thinking about his rare and precious father, then watched Baba eat until he was satisfied that he had enough.

15

Julien

Julien left Baba resting and crouched down in their yard under the gnarled tree. Its branches were twisted, as if it wasn't sure which direction it was meant to grow. There were burls on its limbs and its leaves were somewhat patchy, but it produced both shade and a lovely deep sound. Julien had always loved it.

He ate the few bites of bread porridge that were left, then pulled the smallest breadcrumb that could still be considered a crumb from his pocket. He put it on his palm and held his hand out, hoping. Every night he did this, certain that the bird that lived in the tree would bring him luck for healing Baba if only he could feed it.

The bird fluttered down, landing nearby. It cocked its head, staring at Julien with one eye.

Julien crooned to the bird. "Take the crumb, little bird. Come. Eat. I will not harm you."

The bird hopped a bit closer.

Julien barely breathed. The crumb was all he could spare. In fact, it was more than he could spare, really, but some things he needed more than food. His arm ached from holding so still, and he chided himself for not having the foresight to prop his hand on his other arm. "Come, little bird," he whispered. "Come eat so Baba will get well again."

The bird hopped closer still.

Julien's finger twitched and the crumb rolled on his palm.

The small movement frightened the bird and it skittered away, returning to the gnarled branches of the tree.

Julien sat back on his heels and a puff of dust rose around his feet. Someday he would make friends with this bird. He would train the bird and it would come when he whistled. It would eat from his palm. It would perch on his head. He would sing to it and it would sing back. He smiled at his dream, then frowned. The way things were going, it might take him his whole life to get the bird to trust him—longer, because he needed to spend his days collecting botanicals for the makers. And by that time, Baba might not need his wish anymore.

He decided to try again, this time with his arm propped. Julien settled down and put his arm against a large stone. The breadcrumb was perfectly placed in the center of his hand. He waited for the bird to become curious again. In a few moments, he heard rustling in the leaves, the fluttering of its small wings as it flew closer. One branch closer. Then another. Finally, down to the ground in front of him.

This was it! Julien knew it. The bird was about to take the crumb when a loud noise startled him and up he flew, into the dusk, leaving Julien alone with his hope and breadcrumb.

The clatter came from down the street: horses' hooves, men's voices, the clanking of metal on metal.

"Almus!"

Uneasiness slithered through Julien. Almus was Baba's name. He ran inside hoping these men were seeking some other Almus. In the dim light, Julien could see Baba sitting bolt upright with a confused look on his face. Why were these men looking for Baba?

Baba grabbed Julien and pushed him into the space under the table, but the boy clutched at his sleeve. "Stay here," he said. "And don't say a word."

Before Julien could respond, they heard the clatter stop outside their home.

Julien faded into the shadows of the corner, inching deeper under the table.

A man burst into the small dwelling, though Julien could not see him from where he was. Baba pulled himself to standing.

"Florian," he said with a touch of uneasiness in his voice. "What is the matter? Are you in need of more echinacea?"

The man chided him, "I wouldn't buy more botanicals from you if you were the last collector in Antiquitilla."

Baba sank back down. "I don't understand."

"Your last batch of elecampane was laced with ragwort. The woman who bought it gave it to her calf for respiratory problems, and instead of healing it, she poisoned it. You know that's an offense worthy of conviction."

"But who would confuse elecampane with ragwort? The only similarity is that they're both yellow."

"Someone who is clever would never confuse them. It's the mistake of a novice," Florian said coldly.

"I would never mistake the two! You know that!"

"You were the last person to bring me elecampane. You and your son."

Julien cringed under the table. Had he confused the two? He wracked his mind, but he was certain he had never done such a thing. Elecampane trumpeted and ragwort was so staccato. Besides, even if Julien had accidentally mixed them, Baba was always careful about sorting the flowers before selling them. This man must be mistaken.

"But what about the ragwort?" Baba's voice sounded unnerved. "Who did you buy your ragwort from? Maybe they mixed elecampane with it?"

"But *I* wouldn't have confused elecampane with ragwort. A woman's calf is dead and someone must be blamed. It's not going to be me. You can wait in the prison and make your case before the judge. Where's your son? We can collect him, too."

From under the table, Julien saw fear in Baba's stillness, then he heard the rawness of his cough.

Baba shook his head. "You wouldn't."

"Poisoning cattle because of a collector's negligence is a

serious offense. The Magister Populi's guards are waiting out-side. Let's go."

"Please! I would never mix the two! You know that!"

Julien stayed silent. A beetle scuttled across the dirt floor, heading toward him. He concentrated on its abrupt move-ments so as not to give himself away.

The man prodded Baba. "Out. We'll come back later to get your son."

Baba coughed again. There was little hope he'd leave the prison once inside—and with Baba sick as he was, Julien knew it was likely that he would die there.

The man spat, then grabbed Baba's arm and pulled him to standing. "Enough! We go." He pushed Baba out of their house. "With you out of the way, I can find the silva flower myself," he muttered under his breath. "Clever as ever, old Florian. Clever as ever."

16

Julien

Though Baba told Julien to stay under the table, Julien couldn't watch while Baba was taken to prison for something he didn't do. He leaped up and grabbed the kettle, still warm from its perch by the fire, and flung it at the man's head.

With impeccable timing, Florian turned to see who or what made the noise behind him. His eyes registered surprise a split second before the kettle connected with the side of his head. He cried out, alerting the guards, but Julien was gone. He'd heard the whistle of the kettle as it sailed through the air and knew that it would strike true. Diving for the window at the rear of the stone cottage, Julien shimmied through it before Florian could even cry out—and long before any guards could react.

Julien somersaulted onto the ground, popping up five feet away as a guard stuck his head out the window. There was an old crumbling wall separating their tiny yard from the alleyway where everyone threw their garbage: kitchen scraps, offal, sewage. Julien vaulted over the wall easily and serendipitously landed on the back of a goat scavenging the kitchen scraps. The goat let out an alarmed cry and took off running, Julien hanging on with determination.

The guard had no hope of catching a goat that had bolted in fear. That, of course, didn't mean that Julien was free and clear. On the contrary, a different man, one with the face of a bludgeon, came running after him from the other side of the yard.

"Stop right there!" he called out.

Julien leaped from the goat and darted from one alley to another, putting as much distance between him and the man as he could. The clattering of horses' hooves and swords and Baba's wretched cough faded as he ran farther and farther away.

He ducked under a laundry line and passed a sleeping dog. He dodged into a courtyard and out the other side, all the while listening for pursuit. After so many turns, Julien thought he'd lost the bludgeon-faced man, and slowed to a trot.

Though he thought he was lost, as luck would have it, this last alley led him directly to the gated wall that surrounded the Official Residence of the Magister Populi. Julien would wait for Baba to arrive and rescue him, for the prison lay behind the wall. He just needed to make sure he didn't get caught himself. He hid behind a table of old men playing one final late-night game of disks. Crouched in the darkness, Julien knew that if

Baba was put into prison, he would have to get him out. There was no one else. And Baba's life depended on it.

As he went to stand, he saw the bludgeon-faced man speaking to the guard at the gate. Julien squatted again, and just in time. The bludgeon-faced man turned, scanning the space.

Julien would wait until the area had cleared before leaving his place of safety. All around him came sounds of encouragement. Small nocturnal animals began to stir. Moths flew through the air, seeking light or heat or companionship. In the distance, Julien heard the call of an owl. In seconds, another owl replied. They hooted back and forth, their call a balm to Julien, a reminder of those nights when he and Baba slept in the woods while collecting botanicals.

As Julien waited, his eyes grew heavy. It had been a long day and he had walked far when he had been collecting. Though he pinched himself in the soft part of his arm and bit the inside of his cheek to stay awake, his head sagged and he fell asleep.

While he slept, the guards brought Baba through the gate to the prison.

While he slept, the men finished their game and, one by one, returned home.

While he slept, the moon rose.

A great *clang* awoke Julien. It was dark, though not as dark as the inside of his home. His neck ached, and his belly felt completely empty. That wasn't a new sensation, but something seemed wrong.

Then he remembered.

Baba.

The man.

The gate!

He launched himself off the ground, stumbled, and fell, rolling in the dust. In one motion, he stood up, ignoring the pain in his left ankle and the blood that seeped from his right knee. How could he have been so stupid as to fall asleep when he needed to be awake? If the gate was closed for the night, he would have to wait for morning when the guards changed and opened the gates for the day. He ran, limping, hoping against hope that he could still get inside. He charged through the open square, but the gate was shut tight.

17

Julien

Julien slapped the wall in frustration. His hand made a satisfying *thwack*. He slapped the stone again.

Something cold and wet touched his leg. Julien jumped, his heart hammering until he realized it was a stray dog. The dog snuffled Julien's hand, as if she hoped something to eat would appear there, and looked at him with hungry eyes that mirrored Julien's.

Julien turned back to the wall and considered scaling it. He had to get inside.

"You! At the wall!" a deep voice called out from the darkness.

Julien froze. The dog's hackles lifted. His options were dwindling. He could run, though his ankle still smarted, and he would inevitably be overtaken by the guard. He could stand still and hope the guard would think he was imagining things.

If he did that, the guard could investigate, and he'd still be caught. Or he could tell the guard his situation. Each of the three scenarios ended up with him in the exact same place: with the guard.

"I say, you there! Stand back!"

The dog let out a low growl.

"And call off your dog."

Julien patted the dog, then stepped away from the wall into view.

"Oh. You're just a pup yourself," the guard said, coming closer. "What are you doing out here so late at night?"

He could lie or he could tell the truth. He was no good at lying—never had been, other than telling Baba he'd had enough to eat. He might as well tell the truth.

"I was trying to find a way to scale the wall."

"Have you got a death wish, my young friend?"

Julien shook his head. "My baba was taken by a man who accused him of something he didn't do and put him in prison."

The guard's face hardened. "Does this man have a flat crooked nose?"

With a start, Julien realized that the bludgeon-faced man who had chased him might have been Florian himself. And he had spent quite some time by the guard, this guard, and it was likely that he had paid the guard to hold Julien for him.

Julien took a step back. "I think so," he said with hesitation.

The guard glowered. "Did his voice sound like wet string?"

"I couldn't say," Julien said. He rotated his left ankle, testing it, in case he needed to run.

"I know this man, and I despise him. His name is Florian. He tells lies, and I hate lies." The guard spit, then stared into space, playing with the handle of his sword as if he wanted to use it on Florian.

But Florian wasn't there, and Julien was. Julien took another step backward.

The guard focused on Julien once more. "If you get to the other side of the wall, you can rescue your father?"

"I hope so."

"And you said your father has done nothing wrong?"

"Baba is an honest man. He has integrity."

"I believe you. Come with me." The guard turned abruptly, his sheathed sword nearly knocking Julien over, and he strode toward the gate.

Was the guard really going to help him? Or was he going to lock him away, too? Julien wished he had run when he had the chance. He followed the guard, and the dog followed him to the massive gates.

The guard stopped and pulled out a key the length of his hand. A smaller door was cut into one of the gates with a series of locks at its right edge. The guard stuck the key into the lock and turned it.

"You and I are on the same side," he said. "We are against this lying man with the crooked nose. He cheated my brother.

I will help you. You go through this door and you are on the other side of the gate. No need to climb. No death wish. Yes?"

Julien was overcome. "Really? You'll let me do that?"

"You are no threat to the Magister Populi. You will find your baba and figure out a plan to free him, though it is not likely you will get him out tonight. Then come back here, and I will let you through if you come before dawn." Here, the guard smiled, his white teeth gleaming in the darkness.

Julien's heart sank, realizing the guard was right; it was not likely that he could free Baba that night. "Do you know where the prison is?"

"Go around to the back. It's at the rear of the grounds, near the rubbish pit. You'll hear the prisoners' moaning, if you don't smell the rubbish first." The guard set about unlocking the rest of the latches. With a final *whump*, he slid the last bolt away from the lock and eased the door open.

"Go, young pup. Save your father."

Julien left the dog behind, slipped through the door, and went into the quiet behind the gates of the Official Residence.

18

Julien

Julien had only been inside the gate once before, years ago when he was little. He didn't remember much of the layout of the grounds, other than they were immense. Consequently, the guard's directions to the prison, such as they were, didn't inspire much confidence. He skirted the wall to the left, keeping to the shadows and walking slowly and soundlessly, for he could not risk getting caught. By the time he made his way around to the back where the prison was, the night was more than half over.

He knew he was headed in the right direction, though, because long before he reached the back, he did indeed hear the prisoners. The air vibrated with their anguish. He listened intently for the familiar sounds of his baba, for the particular beat of his heart, the resonance of his cough, and there it was, tangled in the prisoners' noise.

He ran through the shadows, worried that this short stay in the prison had made Baba even sicker. As Julien ran, the sounds of the prisoners assailed him, and their agony nearly made him drop to his knees.

A window sat high on the side of the prison. The stones of the wall were rough, and Julien began to climb, finding a hand grip, then a place for his foot, one hand, one foot at a time. Slowly, he reached the barred window and called down to the prisoners. "Is there a man named Almus here?"

A few prisoners called out from their places on the stone floor. "Tell my mother I am sorry!" "Get me some water! Water, I say!" "Rip out the heart of Constantine Festus!"

Julien let his eyes grow accustomed to the darkness in the prison and studied their faces. Their voices carried more than words. The clamor spoke of each one's history, his crime, his sorrow.

"Baba?" he called out. "Baba?"

He saw movement below him.

"Julien?"

There was Baba, pale, but very much alive.

"Baba!" Julien was nearly overcome with relief. "I've got to get you out of here. I heard that man say he wanted you out of the way so he could search for the flower."

"I'm not surprised. I know that *I* didn't mix up elecampane with ragwort, and I know that *you* didn't mix them up, so whatever he says, we are not at fault. But that doesn't change our circumstances. Julien, listen to me. You'll need to get a lawyer. The only way you'll be able to do that is—"

"If I find the flower, I know. I *will* find it. I will bring it back, and then the Magister Populi will have to let you out."

Almus began to cough. In between coughs, he said, "Julien—the danger—is great."

"I don't care. Just tell me what I need to know to find it!"

"Yes! Tell him where to find it!" another prisoner said, sounding altogether too interested.

Baba coughed uncomfortably, then continued. "Do you remember where I said it grows? The only place I have never allowed you to go while we were out collecting."

Julien nodded. "I know where you mean."

"Choose your steps carefully and slowly. Stay away from dark areas and brilliant vivid green. You'll know what I mean when you get there."

Julien set his jaw. "I'll be back, Baba. I'll get you out of here."

The prisoners roared, their words a jumble of sense and nonsense, but amid the noise he heard Baba say, "You have been the greatest joy in my life." Julien felt a rush of love for his father. He had to find the silva flower.

19

Una

Cassius led Una out of the Official Residence toward the rear of the grounds. "The horse is outside the wall," Cassius whispered. They did not speak more for fear of being caught by other guards who might question why Una was wandering around so late at night.

Una wished she could escape into the sky, above the scents that hovered near her. The thick wall of baked earthen bricks that surrounded the Official Residence was meant to keep out marauders, mercenaries, and thieves of all kinds, but it also trapped scents. While she loved the smells of the gardens, the smells from the kitchens and rubbish pit were overpowering here.

She followed the shadow of her uncle as they circumnavigated the expansive building of the Official Residence, always moving toward the right. The farther they went, the more putrid the air became. The smell of rotting vegetables and refuse grew so strong that Una paused to bury her face in her arm to breathe. Una wasn't sure she could go on, but she pictured her mother's face. Then she pictured her father's face when he left the room without looking at her. She kept going.

Unfortunately, the path they were on now led toward the large rubbish pit. Una looked at the variety of garbage around her that hadn't made it into the pit, her hand covering her mouth and nose. Heads of chickens, broken pottery, all manner of dirty, slimy, unidentifiable things. She gingerly stepped around the least offensive things and made her way past the pit as quickly as she could, astounded that there would be such filth on her father's grounds.

Cassius paused, scanning their surroundings to be sure, once again, that no one was watching. There was a building to the left with a barred window high up on the wall. A shadow ran to its side. Scuffling noises came from within, and then there was the distant sound of voices.

Una looked at Cassius, frightened. After what seemed like an eternity, but was really only a few minutes, the shadow raced back into the night.

She breathed a sigh of relief. That was a mistake. When she inhaled again, the air was accompanied by the full stench of the rubbish pit. But within that sip of air, she noticed an unexpected scent: love. Surprised, she inhaled a little more. It was similar to her mother's scent, but this love was undercut by worry and fear.

She turned her head, trying to escape the scent's sadness. Yet it drew her toward the building where she'd seen the shadow. Turning to Uncle Cassius, she whispered, "I need to do something. I'll be right back." She could smell his annoyance, but she took off running before he could respond.

20

Una

Una stopped beside the building. The stink of dread and unwashed bodies wafted through the window. But above that smell came the scent of love—love for one's child.

Una's mind told her to return to Cassius, but her heart drew her onward.

She couldn't leave.

Not until she found out what this was all about.

She took a breath through the fabric of her tunic and began the climb to the small barred window.

When she reached it, a man cried out, "Julien? Thank goodness you're back—I forgot to tell you to bring a stick." Before Una could answer, he said, "Who are you? Where's Julien?" A scent of suspicion fluttered from the man, momentarily covering his sorrow, his love.

The other prisoners began grumbling. "Be quiet!" "Water?

Did you bring water?" "May a tree land on the head of your brother's dog!"

The man peered up at the window expectantly.

"I'm—I'm no one important," Una finally said. "And I don't know who Julien is."

"Then why are you here?" The smell of suspicion grew stronger, but an element of confusion was added to it.

"I'm not sure—or rather, it's hard to explain. Outside, in the stink of the rubbish, I smelled love and sadness."

The man sighed, then coughed as if the sigh had been too taxing for him. "You must be very perceptive."

"Can I help you?"

"Probably not. You are just a child, and I am a man without hope."

Una thought. "Perhaps, but I am out here and you are in there."

The man nodded, and Una could see his teeth gleam as he smiled in the darkness.

"Perceptive—and wise." His smile faded as he said, "I am imprisoned because of an unjust accusation, which has left my son on his own."

Ah. No wonder this man smelled of sorrow and lost hope. Una's mind continued to urge her feet to move on, that this man was not her responsibility, but her feet remained rooted at the man's love for his son. "Is there nothing that can be done?"

The man shrugged. "My son has gone to look for the silva flower in the hopes that the reward will be enough to free me."

Una's heart plummeted. The silva flower would get him nowhere. She would not be there to receive it, thus who knew if her father would honor his promise of a reward? Una bit her lip. What could she do? She couldn't go back just to receive the silva flower to help an unknown boy. Cassius would leave without her, and he was the one person who could help her find the scent of her mother. Perhaps she could find the boy before they left the city and give him one of her trinkets that he could sell to hire a lawyer. That seemed like the best alternative. "I may be able to help. Where has your son gone?"

"He'll be at the west city gate. If the gate has already been opened for the day by the time you get there, you should find him on the road to Riddle. Tell him to bring a stick."

The scent of his love for his son grew so strong that it drove out all the foul smells surrounding them, and Una inhaled, gaining strength from it as she hurried on her way.

21

Julien

Ignoring the pain from his left ankle, Julien ran back to the gate where he had entered, filled with worries. His ears rang with the unknown. How could he possibly find this flower? But then, how could he possibly not find the flower? It was the only way to get Baba out of jail.

When he reached the wicket door, he pounded on it. The guard shushed him, hurrying to throw back the locks.

"What of your haste, young pup? Did you find your father?"

"Yes, but I must go!" Julien rushed past the baffled guard, down the street toward the city walls.

As dawn was soon to break, a crowd had begun to gather: a group of laborers headed toward their fields, a merchant on horseback, a woman on a donkey. Someone else pulled a cart.

Each wanted to be headed toward their work by the time the sun rose.

Two guards in uniform stood at this gate. The larger one clinked through a huge ring of keys. A faint rumble of voices came from the other side of the wall as country folk waited to enter the city to set up their wares for market. He heard a jumble of words hinting at the goods they were each selling: turnips, baskets, fish, spun wool. He even thought he heard the old woman who sold soup from her cart singing out something about luck and time. If she was selling luck, Julien would have been her first customer if he'd had any money.

Julien pushed toward the front of the crowd, and as soon as the gray light of dawn touched the city, the guard tucked the key into the lock, twisted it, and opened the gate. Julien was the first through. He shut his ears to angry cries and ran so fast that the noise blurred behind him.

He hurried through the flat fields toward the rising wilderness where a meadow of wildflowers grew. He passed that, ascending until he reached the grove of old sycamore trees where he and Baba had taken shelter the night Baba grew ill. How he wished he could go back to that day to change the outcome!

He couldn't go back, though. He could only go forward, heading into unknown territory. Julien had never been to the bog, and he was searching for a flower he didn't know in a place with dangers that he wasn't familiar with. All this in an impossible time frame to free his father from an unjust imprisonment. His odds were not good.

These were the thoughts racing through his mind as Julien ran toward the bog at the far side of the mountain. He was so caught up in these memories and fears, that he forgot a very important thing—to listen. He missed the warning of a bell. That missed warning cost him, for the bell was on the horse of a marauder. Julien crested the top of a hill and ran into a camp of bandits, right into the waiting arms of their guard.

22

Julien

"What have we here?" the marauder asked. "A boy? Or a large rat?"

Julien fought against the thick arms of his captor. "Let me go!" He tried to kick, but the man simply lifted him into the air, and his feet struck nothing. He twisted left and right, but to no avail. "I'm just collecting botanicals!"

"Really?" a different voice said. "Tie him up and put him in the tent. He might be useful. We'll deal with him later."

As Julien struggled, his captor held his wrists together while someone else trussed him with strips of rough hide. When they finished with his wrists, his captor kicked Julien's feet out from under him. The boy fell hard. His breath was knocked out and he struggled to fill his lungs with air. Pain shot through his tailbone, and the marauders began binding his ankles with more strips of hide.

Though Julien wanted to fight back, there didn't seem to be a point with two grown men against one rather small, almost twelve-year-old boy. He stopped struggling and watched as the guards finished tying him up.

The dimness in the shadowy woods turned everything gray and shrouded their surroundings in obscurity. Though Julien couldn't have given much of a physical description of his captors—other than a long strip of patterned cloth tied around the tops of their heads and an abundance of facial hair on the bottom of their chins—he was able to distinguish among them with his ears.

The man who grabbed him had a surprisingly high voice for one so big. The second man spoke with quick and precise pronunciation, as if he didn't want to waste time or words on unnecessary things. And the third man, the one who had trussed Julien, hadn't said anything, but Julien heard his desire to please the others in the way he rushed to tie up Julien's wrists and ankles.

"That should do it," the third man said.

Before he could stop himself, Julien said, "You sound like a weasel."

The other marauders laughed as if that was the funniest thing they'd ever heard. "Weasel! The name suits you!"

The man took a dirty cloth from his pack and shoved it in Julien's mouth.

"Sound like a weasel, do I? Well, thanks to this, you sound like silence." He heaved Julien to his feet, then pushed him into a tent. It was pitch dark inside, and Julien landed facedown on mats of coarse and dirty fur. Though he felt his cheekbone begin to swell and bruise from the fall, Julien was grateful he hadn't landed on his tailbone again. For that matter, he was grateful they hadn't killed him outright. But what good was that if he was as imprisoned as Baba was? If he couldn't find the flower and save Baba, who would?

Nobody.

Julien's body ached, but not as much as his heart. How could he have been so careless?

As he lay there, each word the marauders spoke outside the tent pummeled his ears, even though they kept their voices low.

"What did the proclamation say about the reward?"

"It said 'greatly honored and greatly rewarded.'"

"What do you think that means? Money? Or power?"

"Or both?" the weasel-voiced man asked, laughing.

Julien twisted until he was on his side, facing the entrance to the tent, and tried, unsuccessfully, to spit out the cloth.

There was silence for a moment, and then the second man—the one who seemed to have some sort of authority—said, "I think it means that whoever finds the flower gets to marry the Magister's daughter."

At that, Julien struggled to sit up. They were talking about the night-blooming silva, the same flower that he needed to free his father. How could he have been so stupid? The Magister's proclamation was sent to all the people of Antiquitilla.

He would not be the only one searching for the flower; anyone who heard that proclamation could be searching for it as well.

Baba had been right. This was no small task. And what was worse, even if he found the flower, he didn't want to marry the Magister's daughter! He wanted to get his father out of prison, so what good would finding the flower be if the reward was marrying some girl?

The men argued back and forth, and Julien began to wish the cloth in his mouth was instead divided between his ears so he could think clearly about what he should do next.

The Weasel spoke. "If we get the flower, who's going to marry the girl?"

"No one, you idiot! The flower won't matter if my younger brother has been successful with his plan. We'll have the girl and make the Magister pay ransom."

Julien began to feel sorry for this girl. He pulled at the bindings around his wrists. All he managed to do was tighten them further. If only he had a knife or a sharp stone.

"And if he doesn't bring the girl?" the Weasel asked. "What then?"

"Then we'll hunt for the flower."

"What do you want to do with the boy?" a new voice asked.

"I haven't decided yet," the man with clipped pronunciation said.

Julien could hear the power in his voice and the strength of his blood. It frightened him in a way that Julien had never been frightened before.

The man continued speaking. "Either we let him join us or . . . we don't."

At that, the men broke into loud laughter.

Julien didn't like the sinister undertone of the man's voice. He didn't want to join the marauders, but the alternative didn't seem like a good option, either. He hoped they would just let him go.

"Cassius's message said it would be today. We shouldn't have much longer to wait. Until we find out about the girl, let's just hang on to him. He may be useful if we need to hunt for the flower. But if my brother has the girl, we'll get the ransom, and no flower needed."

About twenty seconds passed before the tent opened and the leader slipped inside.

As the man let his eyes grow accustomed to the darkness within, Julien listened to his sounds. A braided vibration of muscle, a staccato pulse, a slight whine as threads stretched in his tunic. It all added up to a very real threat, and Julien nearly shook with fear.

"Today is your lucky day." The man took the rag out of Julien's mouth.

Julien's tongue felt thick and swollen, and refuting the man seemed both unwise and more than he could manage, so he said nothing.

"You're going to join us. Common sense tells me that you must have some useful skills if you're out collecting in the wilderness on your own."

Julien realized he had to say something, even if it wasn't very much. "I only collect ordinary botanicals for the makers in the market." His words, though slightly slurred from the gag, were clear enough.

"Good." The man took out a knife and tested its sharpness against his thumb. "You will help us find a special flower."

"But I only know where common flowers are," Julien said.

"You can think about where the uncommon ones might be until you do know." The man kicked him in the gut.

Once again, the new pain in his side coupled with the old pain in his tailbone couldn't compete with the pain in his heart.

23

Una

When Una had returned to where Cassius hid in the shadows at the Official Residence, she could tell he was cross, but he said nothing. He simply led the way from the rubbish pit to the gate in the wall. There, at the gate, the guard was asleep, just as Cassius had said.

Una turned back to look at the Official Residence. This was the farthest she'd ever been from it by herself. It gave her a funny feeling inside, guilt and uncertainty, and maybe a little fear, too. Then she remembered how her father hadn't even looked at her when the messenger came to announce the birth of the baby, and her resolve steeled. They continued walking without speaking, turning left, then right, then left again until they came to a curving road that smelled strongly of horses.

They picked up a sad, swaybacked little mare laden with saddlebags full of provisions, and headed for the western city gate. Una kept her head low, mimicking the servant girls she'd seen so she wouldn't arouse any suspicion, but she kept watch for a boy. She inhaled deeply, certain his scent would give him away; undoubtedly it would match the scent of his father. But she caught neither scent nor sight of him.

This was probably just as well. She had not yet told Uncle Cassius about the man in the jail. If they didn't find the boy, then she wouldn't have to explain herself to her uncle. She also wouldn't have to explain herself to the boy, who had no knowledge of her conversation with his father and was certain to be suspicious of a stranger giving him trinkets.

The mare slowed as they reached the city limits. It was early, but the city gates had already opened and crowds of individual scents swarmed her. A messenger boy rushed past with a tray of bowls holding steaming liquid. Una took a quick sniff. Spice. She closed her eyes and took another sniff. A hot tang. She smiled. How welcome a bowl of steaming broth made with spice and hot tang would be. When she opened her eyes, the boy was gone, and a tall woman holding a jug on her head hurried by.

The guards' attention was focused on the crowd entering the city, so uncle and niece slipped past them unnoticed. It was so easy that Una nearly laughed out loud, but her heart reminded her there was nothing funny about a dead mother and a father with a new wife and baby. There was nothing funny about an extended family that had been kept from her. There was nothing funny about a man jailed unjustly and a boy on a quest that was doomed to fail.

She walked out of the city behind the swaybacked mare and Uncle Cassius. There was so much energy here. She knew little of the city beyond the Official Residence, and absolutely nothing outside the city walls. She had once asked Ovid what was out there.

"Nothing for you to concern yourself about, my little flower."

"But what's there?" she insisted.

"Only the land of Riddle, a place of wanderers and outlaws."

At the time, Una was certain that the title of wanderer and outlaw was given to people who went around teaching the law outside the city walls. Now she was pretty certain that was wrong.

Una took in the landscape. To the west was a narrow but well-packed road leading to large plots of farmed fields. She assumed that would be the way Cassius led them. Their ancestral home would undoubtedly be within the rich agricultural lands. To the north, another road led toward hills at the base of mountains. If she were looking for a rare flower, it wouldn't be among the well-tended agricultural lands. It would be too obvious among rows of fruit trees and fields of grain. The boy must have headed north. The realization hit her with a surprising disappointment. Never had she been able to do anything of great use in her whole life. Never had she done something good for another person. Here had been her chance, and she found herself sorry that it would come to nothing.

But instead of turning west, Cassius turned north.

"Uncle Cassius," she said to get the young man's attention.

"Hmm?"

"Are we going the right way?"

"Yes, my home is beyond the mountains. That is why I could not come visit your mother when I was younger. The way is steep and sometimes dangerous."

Una fingered the strap on her pack. If they were going north, maybe she could find the boy after all.

The road started flat, uncluttered by rocks or hazards. The mare kicked up clods of dirt that occasionally spattered Una's legs. As they moved farther and farther from the city, the land grew rockier and began to rise into foothills.

Una lifted her head to the misty sky. The morning light was still gray, and the mountains seemed as far away as ever. The Official Residence seemed even farther away. Everyone would probably still be fast asleep, but oh, the excitement there would be when she was found missing! Ovid's face came into her mind and she felt a twinge of guilt, for he would be under condemnation because of her absence. She really should have left a letter. She just hoped her father wouldn't be angry with him. It wasn't Ovid's fault that she had left. On the contrary, it was mostly her father's fault.

Una took a deep breath, seeking the scent of love. Everything would be all right. It had to be. She would find the boy so he could help his father, and she would make a new home for herself with her mother's family. Both of them would find exactly what they hoped for.

24

Una

They began climbing a low hill when a scent caught Una's attention. It was a faint scent, reminiscent of love and worry and fear, but it was enough. Una knew this must be the boy. The scent was coupled with rumbling voices that somehow smelled dangerous. Una wondered if they belonged to wandering outlaws from the land of Riddle, and if so, was the boy among them?

"Uncle Cassius!" she whispered fiercely. "Uncle Cassius!"

He didn't seem to hear her and continued onward.

She listened as hard as she could, but couldn't distinguish any specific words until one of them said, "What do you . . . with the boy? . . . flower needed."

Her ears perked up. *Boy? Flower?*

But the next words made her blood go cold. ". . . Younger brother . . . his plan . . . the girl . . . get the ransom."

The girl? Ransom? Could these men be talking about her?

Why wasn't Uncle Cassius making any attempt to avoid whomever was on the road? "Uncle Cassius!" she hissed once more, a little louder this time.

The third time was the charm, because Cassius turned around. Instead of exhaustion or ignorance, she saw excitement radiating from his eyes. "What is it?" he asked.

"It sounds as if there are men ahead."

"Yes, Una, there are, and if I'm correct, they are my brothers!"

A seed of apprehension took root inside Una. Cassius's brothers? Ransom? Her worry grew like an invasive weed as she realized she truly knew nothing about this uncle of hers. She had trusted him because he bore a resemblance to her mother and his scent seemed related to hers. Was he really even her uncle? She took a furtive glance at him, uncertain.

It was then that her apprehension blossomed into fear. No one at the Official Residence knew where she was. They might not even realize she was gone yet. Now she really wished she had left a letter for Ovid.

Una took stock of what she had in her pack that might prove useful. There wasn't much. The collection of scents was no weapon. Her gardening trowel and clippers were a little better, but not much use against several men with malice in their plans. Her best protection was a small knife. Nothing else she carried would serve any purpose but for her own comfort, which was of little worth if she were held for ransom. Even the mare in front of her was so old that it would never outrun any other beast, let alone a quick man.

So that left her with her wits, and possibly the boy. If these men had the boy, perhaps he might help her. But for now, she had to do the unexpected, and she had to do it soon.

While Uncle Cassius's attention was riveted on the camp up ahead, Una stopped walking and slid behind a tree. She waited for a moment to see if Cassius noticed, but he continued toward the men and their conversation about ransom.

She crept toward another tree so she could watch Cassius's progress and so she could see what she was up against. There was a small camp just within the cover of the trees. A few large, hairy men. A single fire. Six horses with jingling bridles. One tent.

The boy must be inside the tent.

She watched as the men heard Cassius approach. He hailed them, and when they were turned toward Cassius, Una made her move. Her nighttime wanderings in the Official Residence had made her practiced at walking silently, at hiding, at not drawing attention to herself, and she approached the tent without any of them knowing.

25

Julien

As Julien sat in the dim tent, every thread of hope he had unraveled. There was no possible way he could free himself, let alone free his father. He sat, utterly wretched, and listened to the men outside as they built up their fire and sizzled meat over the flames. Julien thought of how long it had been since he had meat, and his stomach growled, betraying him.

In the midst of all this there came a stillness. The sounds of the forest quieted, as if they were swept into a cloth bag and cinched shut. Birds stopped chirping, and even the breeze died. Then came the sound of footsteps and the *clip-clop* of hooves.

Julien wished he could see outside the tent. Perhaps someone was coming to help him? More likely, more men were returning to the camp.

The footsteps stopped, the horse whinnied, and the silence deepened.

The leader spoke a single name. "Cassius?"

A new voice said, "Brutus!"

Rejoicing commenced with hooting and hollering. Julien crawled like a caterpillar to the edge of the tent to see what was happening. The leader of the marauders held a younger man in an embrace, slapping his back. The others gathered around them with joyful looks on their faces.

Julien didn't know what the arrival of this new person meant, but it was a diversion. He felt for the bottom of the tent, wondering if he could slide underneath and sneak out, but he was halted by the stakes holding the tent down.

As he sat there, a *scritching* noise came from the rear of the tent. Julien shifted to look. The tent wall jiggled. As he watched, a knife sliced through the hide and began cutting downward in a very careful and nearly silent manner. Julien wriggled his way closer.

The knife disappeared and then reappeared about two feet away to make another cut, parallel to the first. Before he could say or do anything else, the flap lifted and a girl peeked through the hole. "Good," she whispered. "You're here."

Just then, a cry came from the newcomer by the fire. "Una! Una, where are you?"

The girl froze. Julien didn't trust the oily sound of the new voice. "Get in here," Julien urged.

She slid through the opening she had cut, and curled into a ball behind Julien. Julien made himself look as big as he could to hide the girl in case someone peeked inside the tent.

More voices joined in calling her name.

Then Cassius said, "She was just here. She can't be far."

"Spread out and search for her. Someone check the tent."

Swift footsteps crossed to the tent and the newcomer's face appeared. In the dim light, he never saw the girl or the slit in the back of the tent.

The man growled and ducked back outside. "She's not there."

Julien felt tugging on his bindings, and then a ticklish sensation across the back of his hand. His bindings gave way. The girl had freed his hands, but she paused as the leader said, "Spread out and look for her. We can't get the ransom if we don't have the girl."

Quickly, she began sawing at the knots that bound Julien's ankles, deftly cutting the strips of hide. In moments, Julien's feet were free.

"We need to leave," she said. "There's a tree right outside. We can climb it and wait them out."

Julien rubbed his wrists and ankles where the hide had bit into his skin, and nodded, hoping his limbs still worked after having been tied up.

"Follow me," she said, once the way was clear. She shimmied out the back of the tent and climbed the tree as silently as a spirit. Julien crept after her.

26

Una and Julien

The living scent of the tree led her upward, higher and higher, until they were far above the tent, far above the fire and the stench of the men and their roasting meat, until the air they breathed was so clear that the only other scent Una detected was that of the boy's love for his father.

When they were safely tucked in among tree limb and leaf, Julien whispered, "Who are you? Why did you rescue me?"

Una bit her lip. She had known this question was coming, but she wasn't sure how to answer it. "My name is Una. I saw you at the jail. I wanted to know why you were there and went to the window after you left. Your father saw my shadow and thought I was you. He told me your direction because he thought I might be able to help. And I . . ." Her voice trailed off. Oh, this was coming out all wrong.

"Yes?"

"I had a knife with me, and you know the rest."

"But why did you get me out?"

This was the part that Una couldn't answer, for she wasn't sure she could explain her ability with smell. She also didn't want to tell this boy his quest for the silva flower was useless. That seemed almost cruel. "It's complicated."

While Una was unsuccessfully trying to explain her actions, Cassius and the marauders rode straight into a meadow of wildflowers in search of her, their horses' hooves trampling the delicate leaves and petals, crushing them, much the way an apothecary grinds leaves and petals in a mortar with a pestle. But while the apothecary turns his destruction into something beneficial, the horsemen only left a path of wreckage.

The churned meadow released a medley of scents: tallgrass, merriefield, windsock, and, most notably, angel's wings. The scent rolled out in waves—like an ocean, a night sky full of stars, a bolt of cascading silk. It was a scent that the long-dead Magistrix might have enjoyed. The wave rolled onward, spreading out until it climbed a tree where two children hid from a very uncertain future.

27

Una and Julien

The wave hit Una in a collision that nearly knocked her out of the tree. She found herself wrapped in a flurry of scent—including Julien's concern and love for his father—that made her pause. It was so complex that before she could identify one piece of what she was smelling, she was distracted by a new one. Una thought her mother's scent might have been woven into this tapestry, but she hadn't smelled it in so long that she wasn't sure. The possibility filled her with joy. She breathed deeply, trying to pull it from the air and into her lungs, her belly, her fingertips. She wanted the scent of her mother's love to mend her spirit, making her whole again.

But the scent was elusive. It rolled onward, replaced by the smell of the tree. It was over so quickly, Una wasn't sure if she had caught her mother's scent at all. She shook her head and inhaled again.

Nothing.

She pushed away from the bark of the tree, stretching to catch a whiff, but to no avail. Had she imagined it? She sank back and took another searching breath, but there was nothing.

"How many men were there?" Una asked quickly.

"Five, I think."

"Good. That means that they left only one behind."

"Yes, there's only one down there now."

"How do you know?"

"I hear him. He sounds like a clumsy giant looking for you. I expect that he'll be looking for me before too long, too."

They heard a growl and an oath and the smack of an angry hand against the tent.

"Right about now, I would say," Julien finished.

"It's time to go," Una said. "I can't waste any more time. We'll have to outsmart him. That shouldn't be too hard."

Julien sized up Una. "How did you think you could help me?"

The complex scent had vanished and Una was beginning to regret rescuing Julien. "I don't have time to explain right now, and you need to get your father out of jail. As soon as we get down from here, you'll be able to purchase his freedom. But I can't tell you any more now."

Only partially satisfied, Julien nodded. She must know where a silva flower was. "What should we do, then?"

Una grabbed a branch that had several round, green, spiny globes. "Chestnuts."

Before Julien could ask what chestnuts had to do with their predicament, Una had pulled off several and handed them to him. Then she gathered some for herself. "How far do you think you can throw these?"

Julien's eyes widened. "Distraction?"

"Yes—you throw in one direction, and I'll throw in a slightly different direction, then the guard will go chasing after the noise he thinks is us. So how far do you think you can throw?"

"I think I can hit that bush over there." Julien pointed to a leafy bush about fifty feet away. "But probably not farther because I can't get a clear shot."

"Do your best," Una said. She had to find that scent, for she needed to know if it was the scent of her mother. If she didn't track it down, if she didn't know for sure, she would be frozen in a cycle of wishing and wondering up there in that tree.

Julien cradled one of the spiny chestnuts in his hand and peered out at the bush. The weasel-voiced man was looking for them.

"You hit the bush, then I'll aim for that tree over there. Then we'll make a run for it in this direction." Una pointed away from the camp, up the mountain.

"Why that way? Is that the fastest way to the silva flower?"

Una sidestepped his second question. "They won't expect us to go there. We'll circle back around to the city."

Julien nodded, rubbed his thumb against a spine, then lobbed the chestnut up and out. It soared through the air and hit the bush with a *thwack*. It was a perfect shot.

But it didn't attract the guard.

"Try again," Una urged.

Julien took another chestnut and threw it. It came down once more in the center of the bush.

The guard looked up, but didn't take the bait.

Frustrated, Una took one of her chestnuts and threw it with such speed that it hit the tree next to the bush with a *crack*. "Quick! Now you!"

Julien hurled another chestnut at the bush. It whizzed through the leaves, sounding conveniently like a person crawling through the shrubs.

That did it.

The guard perked up and ran for the bush.

"One more for good measure." Una pitched another chestnut a bit farther away. Julien threw another, too, creating a trail of sound for the guard to follow.

28

Una and Julien

Miraculously, Una's plan worked. The guard was off and away. Down they climbed, out of the tree and into the camp. Una pulled out her knife and quickly marked the tree. Even though the scent was not down here, at least she would be able to make her way back to this tree where she discovered it.

Meanwhile, Julien ran to the fire. He grabbed a piece of meat, tossing it back and forth between his hands as he took off up the mountain. Una followed. When the meat was cool enough, he ripped off a piece and gave it to Una. The two ate, creeping through the undergrowth, forging onward through the quiet as far from the path as they dared. They didn't talk, but they each took comfort in knowing that the other was there. Neither of them was alone, and that was a gift Una and Julien both needed.

As they walked, Una secretly tested the air for the right scent, but she always exhaled with disappointment. Only once did they hear the pounding of horse hooves in the distance.

When the land had flattened and the city walls were in sight, when they were far enough away from the marauders to feel safe, Julien cleared his throat to get Una's attention. "So, will you tell me where the silva flower is now?" Julien asked.

Una didn't answer.

"Wait." Julien stopped and tugged on her arm. When she wouldn't look at him, he said, "You don't know?"

Una couldn't bear to lift her eyes to meet his gaze. "The silva flower doesn't matter."

"What do you mean it doesn't matter? My father's freedom depends on me finding that flower!"

"I never said I knew where the flower was," she said. "I told you that you would be able to buy his freedom."

Una pulled off her pack and found the small gold bottle that she had brought to hold her mother's scent. "Take this," she said, putting it into Julien's hands. "It's not much, but hopefully it will help."

Julien's eyes popped. He had never touched gold. In fact, he had only seen it once before when he crossed paths with a very rich man buying a large tear of myrrh from the myrrh vendor at the market. He had caught a quick glimmer as the gold coin exchanged hands. But he had never forgotten that glimmer.

And now he held not just a coin, but a whole bottle made entirely from gold. A bottle with filigrees and patterns all around it. He had never seen such a beautiful container. Its beauty sang.

Una took a deep breath. "The silva flower is meant for me, but I don't want it." Una knew that these words would betray her, but she had to be honest with Julien. She owed him an explanation.

Julien took a minute to process this. His face flattened as understanding dawned on him. "You're the First Daughter?"

Una nodded.

Suddenly, Julien was very aware of his dirty feet and his tousled hair, his skinny arms and his threadbare clothes. He wasn't comfortable in his clothes, and worse yet, for the first time ever, he wasn't comfortable in his skin. Now he knew why Una couldn't bear to look at him.

"The silva flower is meant to be a gift to remind me of my mother, but that's the one flower that my mother really didn't like."

"She liked angel's wings best," Julien said softly.

Una furrowed her brow. "How do you know that?"

"Baba knew your mother. He was her head gardener."

Una's eyes filled with tears at the thought that there were things about her mother that she had not known, things that Una would never have the chance to learn. The unfairness of it ripped into her. That this boy—who hadn't even existed in her world until the previous night—knew her mother's favorite flowers when she herself didn't, made her feel her mother's loss even more keenly. She turned away.

"I'm sorry," Julien said. "Did I say something wrong?"

"No, it's just—my mother died when I was nearly seven, and you knew something about her that I didn't. My memory of her is fading, and that makes me sad. There's a certain scent she had that brings her back to me. I've been searching for it, but I haven't found it yet."

Julien rolled the gold bottle back and forth in his hand. "It seems we're in the same boat. You seeking your mother, and me seeking my father."

"Your father is still alive, though." Una looked at him. "Take the bottle and go." She found this hard to say, since it meant she would be on her own again. She hardly knew Julien, but his presence was different than Ovid's or anyone else at the Official Residence. He was like a friend. A real friend.

Julien's pity grew. He never knew his mother, so he had no memories of her, but he knew how devastating it would be to lose Baba. "I am sorry. Truly I am. But I'm also grateful for your help." He lifted the bottle, then hesitated, wondering if he should stay with her, wondering if there was something he could do to help her the way she was helping him.

"Go," she said. "The gate for the city should be straight ahead."

"What will you do?"

She hadn't thought that far ahead. Her plan had been to meet her mother's family, but it was clear she couldn't go back to Cassius. Perhaps she could find her mother's family on her own? But what if they were all like Cassius? She couldn't bear to think that she was related to such people. That might explain why her mother had never spoken of the family she came from. Why her father had never mentioned the strain between their families. If the rest of the family was like Cassius, Una was better off on her own.

It was also clear that she couldn't return to the city—to the Official Residence—to be alone and ignored until she was married off to some political rival. She didn't want that future.

Finally, she said, "I'm not sure, but I'm not going back yet. At least out here I can make my own choices, like you."

Julien wondered once more if he should stay with her until he was sure she was all right.

But then Una spoke. "You should go."

She was right. He had to get Baba. He had no more time to stay with this strange and generous girl. Julien took one last look at Una, then hurried toward the gate, wishing there was something he could do for her in return.

29

Una

Once Julien was out of sight, Una sat down on a rock. For a short time she had had an uncle, a plan, and a friend. She'd never had a friend before, and now the loss of him compounded all her other losses—mother, father, home, hope. Now she had nothing, and she couldn't go back without something to keep her mother's memory alive.

Her mother's ancestral home might have provided that—some small item from her past, anything that had been her mother's—but now she would never go there. She couldn't trust Cassius, even if he was her uncle. The hope of meeting her mother's family and finding her mother's scent among them had vanished.

The only plan she had now wasn't even a plan. She told Julien she wanted to make her own decisions, but she couldn't even see what options she had.

Her thoughts turned to the wave of scent that had washed over her when she was in the tree. Her mother's scent had been there among all those others, hadn't it? She closed her eyes trying to recreate the peculiar incident. It had been so vivid, like she could reach out and touch it. But no matter how hard she tried, she could smell nothing here but air and dirt and people having come and gone. If she'd smelled her mother's scent, she would have been able to remember it, wouldn't she?

She tried to picture her mother's face instead—the arch in her eyebrow, her soft cheek, the mole by her ear, the light that danced in her eye—but she couldn't hold the vision together. She only had memories of separate pieces and parts—and even those were fading.

Una pushed herself off the stone. There was no point in staying here. Julien wasn't coming back. He would probably get his father out of jail and take him home, where they would no doubt eat a celebratory meal. She wished she could be at their table, carefree and rejoicing over bread or rice, even if the food was scanty. She wished she could ask his father about her mother, about angel's wings, about her garden. But Julien was gone, and she couldn't go back into the city. Not yet.

Una shouldered her pack once more. Maybe she should search for angel's wings. Even if she didn't know exactly what they looked like, she should be able to smell them, she imagined. The thought gave her a sliver of encouragement.

She began retracing her steps up into the hills. The meat Julien had shared with her had been eaten long ago, and she was hungry, so she pulled a dried pear from her bundle and began eating it slowly. She needed to make them last, for night would soon arrive and tomorrow was a new day with new hungers.

She went along, one foot after the other. There was a steadiness in her gait, and the repetition pushed out her uncertainty, making room for confidence. Yes, Una was in a world where she had no experience, but she was a clever girl. With her wits, a bit of food, and the tools she brought, she could doubtless find what she needed, even if she wasn't quite sure what it was yet.

Tonight, she would clip her way into a bower of greenery to sleep, hidden from those who might seek her, and then she would find that elusive scent of her mother, wrapped up in angel's wings.

30

Julien

When Julien left Una, he went straight to the Official Residence. He was afraid that if he tried to sell the bottle, he would be thrown into jail himself, for why would someone like him have a gold bottle? He was sure to be suspected of theft. Then he would be no better off than Baba. No, he had to be careful. Because sometimes, even when you had the best of intentions, luck was not with you.

He did have the best of intentions, though, and he hoped to find the guard who had helped him earlier, the one who hated the bludgeon-faced marauder.

Instead, a different guard stood at the gate.

As Julien approached the guard, he fidgeted nervously and nearly dropped the bottle.

"Where did you get that?" the guard asked, his hand now wrapped around Julien's fist clutching the bottle.

Julien froze, fear drying his mouth. The guard's forearms looked like they were hewn out of stone. Julien didn't know what to do. Why hadn't he kept still? Why hadn't he wrapped the bottle in the hem of his shirt or his sleeve, keeping it safe until the time came to reveal it? He tried to wrench his arm free, but the guard held him tightly, and Julien cried out in pain.

An old man who was speaking to another guard came to investigate. "What is going on?" he asked.

Julien looked from the guard to the old man. Sometimes luck appears in the form of a penny or a shooting star, but serendipity is rarely so concrete. Sometimes serendipity takes the form of an old man with drooping skin and kindness in his eyes.

Trusting the kindness that he saw, Julien took a risk and said the most unusual thing he could have said: "Sir, Una gave it to me so I might have my father released from jail."

The old man gazed at the boy for a moment, then he squeezed his hand. After a nod to the guard, the man said, "Come with me."

Julien followed him.

Once they were away from the guard, the old man spoke softly, "You have seen Una? How is she?"

Julien breathed a sigh of relief. He had hoped this man with the kind eyes knew Una. He relayed the story of his rescue and their evasion of the men, including one named Cassius. He told him of Una's reluctance to return home without some remembrance of her mother and of Una's gift to save his father.

At this the man nodded. "I suspected something like that. I am Ovid. I served Una, and before her, Una's mother. Now, what's this about your father?"

"If you served Una's mother, then perhaps you know my father. He was the head gardener, Almus."

Ovid stopped walking and turned to face Julien. "You're Almus's boy?"

Julien nodded.

"Oh, child! And you say he's in jail? Let's get your father first, then we'll discuss Una."

Julien was so overjoyed that he nearly leaped into the air.

"Your father was the most honest man I've ever known. How did he end up in prison?" Ovid asked as they changed direction.

"A man named Florian accused him of mixing ragwort with elecampane, which then poisoned somebody's calf. But really, Florian just wanted to find the silva flower without competition from Baba."

Ovid *tsk*-ed. "That's just like Florian."

"You know Florian?"

"He was the man who took over as gardener after your father left, but he didn't stay employed long. He's not the man that your father is." Ovid shook his head. "Florian lacked integrity, honesty, work ethic, knowledge. Your father had all that. Florian didn't."

Julien followed Ovid down a gravel path toward the rear of the grounds. His heart grew lighter, knowing his father would be free soon.

He touched Ovid's arm. "Here is the bottle—to pay for all of this."

Ovid pushed his hand away. "You return that to Una. It was her mother's. She should have it."

"You'll still free my father?"

"Yes, of course I will. Almus was a dear friend, and it is the right thing to do."

Ovid spoke to the guard at the jail. Following their conversation, Julien heard the *clank* of keys and the rasp of metal on metal as the lock turned.

Moments later Baba's arms were around him. Julien couldn't keep his tears from flowing, so happy he was to have Baba back.

31

Julien

Not only was it a happy reunion for Julien and Baba, but it was also a happy reunion for Ovid and Baba, as the two friends hadn't seen each other for many years. They embraced joyfully, then Ovid hurried them away from the prison and back to the residence where Ovid and the other servants lived.

"Let's get you cleaned up, Almus," Ovid said. "Some hot water will do you good. And then I'll bring you something to eat and some tea—horehound, from the sound of it."

Julien could hear the fierce rattle in Baba's lungs and the way he struggled to get his breath. He listened to the air wrestle its way in and out. The sound was different than it had been before. It was worse—far worse. Julien shut out the sound by relating the story of his capture by the marauders and how Una rescued him.

Baba's eyes twinkled, delighted with Una's spunk. "I can't

believe she did such a thing. Where could she have gotten a gold bottle?"

"Oh! She's the First Daughter."

"That's who I spoke to at the window of the prison?"

Julien nodded.

"But what was she doing out in the middle of the night?"

Julien told them of Una's desire for a specific scent—the scent that reminded her of her mother.

Baba's eyebrows rose, and he leaned forward. "A scent that reminded her of her mother?"

"Yes."

"Did you tell her about angel's wings?"

"Yes, of course, but neither of us knows what they look like."

"We must bring her to the field of angel's wings."

By this time, the group had reached a room with flagstones on the floor and a large metal tub.

"As much as I want the First Daughter's happiness, you're not going anywhere, Almus," Ovid said. "I'm going to heat some water. The steam will help your breathing and then you can get some rest. Julien will help Una."

For the first time, Julien felt as if the responsibility of his father's health wasn't entirely on his shoulders.

Ovid filled the large metal tub with hot water and a few sprigs of rosemary. "I should tell the Magister Populi about Una, but I think she needs a little more time on her own. I'll go make some tea now and put together some supplies for Julien, though I think it would be best if he set out first thing tomorrow morning. You will, of course, stay in one of the extra rooms down the hall."

Baba started to decline, but he was overtaken by a coughing fit.

Ovid looked toward Julien, who nodded, worried.

Ovid left, and Julien helped his father out of his clothes, then turned to the corner where a smaller washtub stood. He filled it with a few pitchers of hot water, then began scrubbing the dirt of the prison off Baba's pants and shirt, soaping and scrubbing and changing the gray water while Baba soaked.

Julien could hear Baba's lungs loosen the longer he relaxed in the hot water, but it wasn't enough. He heard both sloshing and a sound like breaking glass when Baba inhaled. Julien scrubbed the pants even harder, as if that would renew Baba's strength. If it could have, Baba would have been the healthiest person in the city.

When Ovid returned, he brought clean clothes for Baba, along with a tray of tea and a plate of small puffy rolls. "Now I'll go put together some things for Una and Julien. I will come back to check on you in a while."

Julien set Baba's sopping clothes to the side and picked up the teapot. He poured a cup for Baba, handing it to him. Baba took the tea gratefully and drank it down.

"Would you like a roll?"

"No, thank you, just the tea. You eat them."

Julien knew Baba was trying to get him to eat, and he did

not want to argue with him. Julien would eat one to satisfy Baba, then save the rest for when Baba was out of the bath.

He took a bite. Julien forced himself to eat it slowly, to savor the light texture rather than gobble it down. It was so different from the coarse bread they normally ate. It was the most delicious thing he'd ever eaten.

When he finished the roll, Julien licked a few stray sesame seeds off his fingertips and returned to the wet clothes. He took the pants, folded them in half, then in half again, and twisted them around and around to wring out the water.

Baba smiled as he sipped the hot tea. "You are so good, dear Julien. Your mother would be so proud of who you've become."

At the mention of his mother, Julien thought of Una and her mother. His face must have shifted because Baba said, "Does it bother you to hear of her?"

"No. It's just . . ." He set the pants to dry and picked up the shirt. "Una. I can't help but think of her and her mother."

"We'll help her find some angel's wings. We must—I owe her my life. Yours, too."

"I don't know what angel's wings look like, though."

"They're about the size of rockrose, but they're individual plants rather than a bush, and when they are small, the leaves look like angel's wings. They grow quickly with large clusters of tiny white flowers that sometimes overshadow the leaves. Go past the chamomile field. They often grow in that pocket of fertile land on the opposite side of the creek, not far from where the rockrose grows. Check there first."

Ovid returned once more carrying a large sack filled with dried pears, pistachios and walnuts, three large cucumbers, and a flask of loganberry juice. "For my small blossom," he said, handing the sack to Julien. "And for you. There's also a pot in here and a flint and steel in case it gets chilly at night. I am too old to go on such a journey, and I have other responsibilities here. You must take care of each other until she sees fit to return home."

Julien nearly laughed. "Sir, I don't think she needs anyone to protect her. She's the one who rescued me."

"Nevertheless, it's good to have an ally."

Julien swung the sack over his shoulder onto his back. It was nearly as large as he was. "Thank you, Ovid. I'll do my best."

32

Una

When Una awoke, it took several minutes to float up from the unconsciousness of sleep to grasp where she was. Her head rested on a net of branches within the protection of a large flowering bush. She wasn't surprised to wake up amidst leaves; she had spent enough time in the courtyard garden at home. What was unusual was the change in scent. None of the regular scents of the Official Residence were present: the heavy smell of breakfast, the clean smell of the washing, the syrup smell of Ovid. Only the smell of branches and leaves surrounded her, sunshine and clouds above, dirt and moss below.

It should have been delightful to wake up in a flowering bush, but the memory of the previous day pushed through and she felt the losses keenly. She was tempted to stay in this place with its pleasant air and shade. But if she stayed here, how would that be any different from her life at home? She still wouldn't have her mother. Her father still wouldn't see her for who she was. It would be harder here—not easier, not better—because here she needed to find water and food, too. Neither of those necessities would be handed to her.

And there were angel's wings to find.

She rose from her bower, picking out a few stray leaves that stuck in her coarse hair. How hard would it be to find some angel's wings? While it was true that she had spent most of her days unsuccessfully tracking her mother's scent, it was also true that she had been limited to the Official Residence. Out here, she should be able to smell them from far off. On the way, she would find water, and maybe some berries, so she could keep the rest of the dried pears for later.

Una began walking, uphill, then downhill, then through some bushes and grass and a patch of light. The scent of growing things showed her the way, beckoning to her until a different scent snuck in. A liquid sort of woodsmoke. On the tail of the smoke came a spice and hot tang. This scent intrigued her. It wasn't the men cooking in their camp. It smelled just like the soup in the city yesterday morning when she and Cassius left. Her stomach felt very empty. But this seemed promising. Better than berries, even.

Una's feet turned toward the spice and hot tang. She followed it around boulders as big as she was and then across a stream. On the other side of the stream, just at the edge of the trees, she saw a wooden cart that held a big pot. Underneath it were some glowing coals. Steam rose from the pot as an old woman with a lopsided bundle of white hair on top of her head stirred the contents. Behind her was a small stone hut.

Una hung back, feeling uncertain about asking for food. This woman looked so poor that Una's dried pears made her feel rich. As she remembered the pears, she wondered if she could trade some for whatever the woman was cooking.

Una stepped out from behind the greenery, and the woman jumped.

"I didn't mean to startle you," Una said.

The woman laughed, her wide lips opening into a bright smile. "No harm done, child." She studied the girl, tipping her head to the side. "You look a bit peaky."

Without meaning to, Una looked at the pot in the fire.

"Wait one moment." The woman rooted around in the cart and pulled out a chipped enamel bowl. "You need soup."

Una nodded. "Yes, please."

The woman dipped her ladle into the pot and poured some soup into the bowl. "I am Vita," she said, handing the soup to Una.

"I'm Una." She took the bowl and raised it to her face. The scent was so strong that it brought tears to her eyes. "What is this?"

"My special recipe. It brings life when it's needed. Looks like you need some."

Una nodded and sipped gratefully, feeling the spice burn down her throat and into her belly. When she spoke next, it was with the exhale of the fire that she had just consumed. "Thank you," she said, certain that the words were flames in her mouth. She had never felt so alive.

Vita sat on a rock. "Now, tell me, why is it that you are here so early in the morning?"

Though Una had never seen this woman before, she had the sense that she could tell her anything, and she found herself wanting to tell her everything. "I'm not sure where to begin," Una said.

"Well, I always try to begin at the beginning, but sometimes beginning at the end is easier."

Una took another sip of the broth and tried to grab hold of what might be a beginning, but decided the ending might be an easier place to start. So she told Vita her story, working her way backward, though it both ended and began with the scent of her mother, the scent of an angel. "I'm sorry my story is so mixed-up."

Vita laughed. "It wasn't mixed-up at all. I understand perfectly. I, too, lost someone when I was very young, and have wished my whole life for a remembrance of him." Her face clouded briefly. When Una put her hand over Vita's, Vita simply squeezed it and stood.

"I need to get to the market to sell my soup. No soup, no customers. No customers, no money. No money, no more soup. With soup comes life!" Vita stirred the pot on the cart one last time. "You will come with me today, I think."

Una wanted to laugh at how she had avoided returning to the city with Julien, and now Vita was suggesting that very destination. But Una found herself wanting to go with Vita, at least for a little while. It felt like the right thing to do, and maybe if she was lucky, she'd find angel's wings on the way. So the two set off, Vita leading the way and Una pushing the cart.

33

Una

Una was surprised at how heavy the cart was, and wondered how Vita pushed the cart on her own every day, especially when the wheels came upon a stone or a large tuft of stubborn grass.

Vita recited quietly, "Soup of life has spice and lime, chiles, garlic, luck, and time."

"Is that what's in your soup?" Una asked.

Vita looked up, as if surprised to see that she was not alone. "Oh, dear child, I forgot you were with me. Though how could I forget, since I'm not the one pushing the cart?"

Una smiled at the older woman.

Vita didn't answer Una's question about the soup. Instead, she asked, "Do you know what I thought you were when you popped out of the woods like you did?"

"What?"

"A *kitsune*!"

Una looked confused.

"A fox fairy," Vita said.

Una shook her head, never having heard of a fox fairy, and laughed at the thought that she could be any kind of fairy. "I guess I really did startle you."

"I was going to ask you where to find the foxfire as St. John's Day is coming up."

"What's foxfire?"

"You don't know the stories about foxfire?"

Una shook her head.

"Everyone should know about foxfire, because everyone could use a treasure—everyone except perhaps the Magister Populi, although I suspect even he has some wishes."

Una stumbled at the mention of her father. "What is foxfire?" she asked again.

"Foxfire is a light in the wilderness that marks the place of a treasure. It's said that the fox fairies leave the light, but that its treasures can only be taken on St. John's Day. I've never seen any foxfire myself, but I've heard of others who have, although they've never seen it on St. John's Day," Vita said, laughing.

Before long, the gates of the city loomed before them. Una ducked her head as they approached the guards, hoping against hope that no one would recognize her. She was grateful once more that she wore sensible and plain clothes so she wouldn't be likely to attract attention.

Vita hailed the guards.

"I see you have a young helper today, Mistress Soup Maker," the younger guard said. "And a right pretty one, too."

Una ducked her head even more, desperately wanting to be invisible and second-guessing her choice to stay with Vita.

Vita simply said, "Good morning to you," nodded at the guards, and led the way as Una pushed the cart through the gate.

The guard said nothing more, and the two passed into the city.

Now that she was inside the city walls again, her thoughts turned to Julien. She wondered if he had been able to free his father. She tried to imagine their happy reunion. She tried to picture their faces, but all she could conjure was the memory of his father's love.

Vita said, "You're quiet, child."

When Una didn't respond, Vita stopped and gazed into the girl's eyes. "I see your concern. You worry about your friend. Set my cart here. I will bring my soup to market. You must find your friend and his father."

Touched by her perception, Una clasped Vita's bony hands, her skin soft and wrinkled. "I *am* worried. If for some reason he wasn't able to get his father out of jail, he might need help. Will you be all right?"

The woman smiled. "Of course. I've walked this path for decades. And should I have the need, another will come along to help me."

"Then I will go. I hope our paths cross again."

Vita squeezed Una's hands. "I hope so, too."

Una hurried off, taking one last look over her shoulder at the woman who had quickly become dear to her, like the grandmother she had never had.

In a city of this size, Una knew finding Julien and his baba would be a challenge, if not nearly impossible. She had no idea where to look, no idea where they lived, no idea if Julien had even been successful in freeing his father. Not to mention, she didn't know the streets and alleyways of the city at all, so even if she did know where Julien lived with his father, she'd never be able to find her way there. As it happened, though, she didn't need to look for them, because Julien found her.

34

Julien

While Una had been wheeling Vita's cart toward the city gate, Julien had been making his way to the city gate as well, straight from the Official Residence laden with the sack from Ovid. He hoped Baba would rest and regain some strength with Ovid tending to him. He hoped he could find Una, though she could be anywhere on the mountain by now. He hoped they would be able to find the angel's wings so he could tell Baba he had helped her. He hoped that angel's wings were the scent Una was looking for.

As these hopes tumbled through his mind, he thought he saw Una standing off to the side of the street, but he knew he must be mistaken. She wouldn't be here in the city. Besides, this girl looked unsure of herself. Una didn't seem like she was anything other than confident.

He looked closer. This girl wore the same sort of trousers that Una had worn.

It *was* Una. He called out to her.

Una jumped, but when she saw the voice belonged to Julien, a huge smile lit her face.

"What are you doing here?" he asked.

She laughed. "I was going to look for you. I wanted to make sure you were able to help your father."

"Yes, thanks to you."

"Where is he?"

"I left him with Ovid. And look!" Julien turned to show the pack on his back. "Ovid sent all this food!"

"Ovid? You saw Ovid?" Una cried out.

"Yes. It was the luckiest thing. He was at the gate looking for news of you when I arrived. He saw the bottle in my hand and recognized that it was yours. And he even knew my father from when Baba was head gardener. So he got Baba released faster than I thought possible." Julien handed the gold bottle to Una.

"That's wonderful!" Una was truly happy that his problem had been solved so quickly, but it left her feeling adrift. What should she do now? She shuffled one foot awkwardly while rolling the bottle between her fingers. "So you'll go home?"

"Go home? No. Baba would not rest until I promised that I would help you find your mother's scent."

"Really?"

Julien laughed. "Yes, really."

Una could not say how relieved she was. "Thank you."

"Besides, we have all this food—enough to last us for some time."

Una bit her lip. "Do you think we'll be able to find it?"

"We have to."

"All right. So . . . where should we go?" Una glanced from left to right and noticed that there were several people taking an interest in them and their conversation.

Julien noticed as well, because one of those people was the bludgeon-faced man. Julien grabbed Una's hand and ran.

35

Florian

Though Florian had never seen the girl, he knew who Julien was: the boy behind the tossed kettle. Almus's son. In the light of day, he bore a strong resemblance to his father. And though he didn't know Una, he sensed that standing before him was opportunity. Opportunity dressed in expensive linen, wearing polished leather boots. Opportunity and her less fortunate friend, who wore rags.

Florian reminded himself that that's where he would soon be, too, if his plans didn't work out. The fact was, he owed money—a lot of it—to Brutus, the marauder who had captured Julien. Florian needed to find the silva flower to pay off his debt, which was why he had Julien's father tossed in jail. Of all the gatherers in the city, Almus was the only one who would have any hope of finding the silva flower. Florian needed to get him out of the way so he could find it first.

He was going to toss the boy in jail, too, but perhaps he

needed to adjust his plan. These were new circumstances, and he was not one to look a gift horse in the mouth. It was likely that the boy would go searching for the silva flower. In fact, Almus might have told him where it was. Florian would simply follow the two and see where it led him.

And even better, the girl looked promising. Quite possibly she had an expensive bauble or two that she might be convinced to hand over. A little extra money couldn't hurt.

"Florian, you are brilliant," he said to himself. "Florian, you are the most ingenious, the most clever, the most . . ." But he couldn't come up with another description. He thought for a moment more, then said, "Florian, you are sharp as a tack."

He just needed to steer clear of their line of vision, trail behind them, and, when the silva flower appeared, relieve them of it.

These were the thoughts that went through his mind as he stood there watching them. When they saw him and bolted, he bolted after them. As the two headed for the gate, he did, too.

Florian was so intent on the path of the two children that he didn't notice a horse-drawn cart headed his way. He couldn't know about the loosened pin on the rear wheel of the cart. He didn't see the uneven cobblestone in front of him. Nor did he realize that the cart contained a fresh load of manure headed to the countryside to cure and be used as fertilizer. If he had a more deserving soul, perhaps someone would warn him about the pin or the cobblestone or the manure. But there were few people in the history of mankind who had a less deserving soul than Florian and—oh dear! What a stink.

36

Vita

Vita, for her part, always went where the wind told her. Mostly, it told her to go to the market, but today, after Una left, the wind blew her toward the Official Residence. Normally, peddlers were not allowed into the grounds of the Official Residence, but the guard who was meant to be at the gate that morning—Cassius—was absent from his post, and in the confusion, no one had been directed to replace him. So Vita sailed through the gates of the Official Residence, the scent of her soup preceding her.

The wind, feeling playful, batted the scent here and there, tossing it high, then swirling it round and round.

Vita called out as she always did, "Soup of life! Soup of life!" And her friend, the wind, did the rest.

Before long, the wind carried the scent of hot tang and spice to one very sick man: Baba.

He sniffed once. Then twice. The smell was invigorating. It woke up his appetite with a roar, which had been, it seemed, in hibernation.

Baba got to his feet and followed the scent until he came to its source: a very old woman, pushing an unusual cart with a big pot of soup.

"You look a bit peaky. Wait just a moment." She reached into the cart to find a cracked enamel bowl. "You need soup of life."

Baba nodded. "Yes, please."

She ladled some soup for him. He inhaled until he filled his lungs with the hot tang and spice, then he lifted the bowl to his lips and drank. The experience was the most unusual he had ever had. His lips, then his mouth, then his throat burned— then constricted—then opened up as the heat of the spicy broth blazed life into him. He gulped down the bowl, until the last drop was gone.

Vita watched as brightness returned to his eyes and his skin lost its ashy pallor. That was the best kind of payment, far better than coins or trinkets, in her eyes. "Feeling better now?"

Baba returned the bowl to her. "Better than I have felt in years. But I have nothing with me to pay you."

"Your renewed health is payment enough." Vita smiled and patted his arm, then carried on, her cart rumbling over the pathways. As she walked on, she cried, "Soup of life! Soup of life!"

Baba really had never felt better. He breathed deeply and felt strength he hadn't felt in years. There was only one thing to do with this newfound health. He turned toward the gates of the Official Residence, bound for the wilderness that enveloped Julien and Una.

37

Una and Julien

Once they were away from the city, and Julien no longer saw Florian behind them, they paused behind some bushes to catch their breath.

"Who was that?" Una asked.

"He's the man who put my father in jail. He's also the man I threw our hot kettle at."

"Did you hit him?"

"I didn't stick around to see, but it sounded like a perfect shot."

"Well done!"

"Yes, except now he's after me. I know my way around this mountain pretty well, though, so I think we can lose him."

Julien went first and he set a quick pace, his bare feet hurrying along the path. He could almost pretend that this was a regular gathering expedition with Baba, except the footfalls behind him were lighter and slightly hesitant, and the pack on his back was heavy with dried fruits, nuts, and the clunk of cucumbers knocking against each other, rather than the sweet whispers of leaves and flowers and the *click* of beads of resin. No, this wasn't like a regular gathering day at all.

It felt strange going up this path with someone other than Baba. It had always just been the two of them together, and occasionally a few goats and their goatherd. When Julien walked with Baba, he often sang as they walked, little songs he made up as they went along, songs about the sound of the insects scuttling under the bark of the terebinth tree or about the melodies of the different places the wind had been. Sometimes he sang about the call of a certain bird as it whistled in the night, or the murmur of moonbeams. Baba never seemed to mind, and it made the time pass for Julien.

He wished he could sing now, something about the hope he heard in Baba's heart, but he felt self-conscious singing in front of Una. She might think he was terrible. She might even laugh. He turned to look at her. She scrambled over a rock, trying to keep up with his pace.

He decided that she wouldn't laugh, but even so, he shouldn't draw attention with Florian searching for them. Instead, he asked, "What will you do when you find your mother's scent?"

Una took a moment before replying. "I'm not sure." She

stepped over a tuft of coarse grass. "I suppose I'll take a sample of it and return home. There's nowhere else for me to go."

Julien felt a twinge of pity for Una.

To be honest, Una felt a twinge of pity for herself, too. She didn't want to think about what she would do afterward. It left her unsettled. Instead, she asked Julien question after question, finding herself unable to stem the tide of her curiosity about Julien and his life, so entirely different from her own.

Julien did not mind her questions—mostly because he was intrigued by the sound of her voice. Sometimes musical, sometimes simply friendly, her voice took his mind off his worries about finding a plant he did not know, about repaying Una for her kindness, about disappointing Baba if he couldn't find the scent, and about Florian following after them.

Una wanted to know everything—what his house looked like, what he ate for breakfast, what his favorite thing was to collect, how they prepared what they collected for market, and if he knew any stories.

Julien dutifully answered her. His house was small. He didn't often eat breakfast, but when he did, it was usually leftovers from the previous day's stale bread. He liked collecting many different things because they each had a challenge to them, and they dried some leaves, crushed and boiled others, and sold some fresh to be distilled at the market. And yes, he knew stories because Baba often told him stories as they walked and worked.

"Will you tell me one?" Una asked.

"I'm sure you've heard them all. They're all common stories."

"I doubt it. When you were hearing stories, I was learning languages and astronomy and the names of generation after generation of influential relatives."

"You make it sound as if all I did was listen to stories while you toiled away with a tutor." Julien gave her a playful shove.

She shoved him back. "It's hard work learning the names of your forefathers sixteen generations back."

"And it's not hard to climb cliffs and collect the tiny flowers—roots and all—that grow in the crevices?"

"Oh, all right, I guess we're even."

"Even?"

She laughed. "You win. Cliff-climbing is undoubtedly harder than memorizing ancestors' names. It's also, I might add, much more exciting."

"Did you really learn your ancestors sixteen generations back?"

Una began reciting, "Claudius Theophilus, Magister Populi XVI, born from Marcellus Claudius, Magister Populi XV, born from Antonius Marcellus, Magister Populi XIV."

Julien interrupted her. "You can stop—I believe you!"

"It wasn't that hard, actually," Una said. "It's tradition to pass on your middle name to your firstborn son."

Julien gave her a sideways glance. "I bet you're glad you weren't a boy. Theophilus?"

Though Una knew Julien was kidding, his words cut her heart.

Julien could tell from the hesitation in her footsteps that he'd said something wrong. "I'm sorry. I didn't mean to make fun of your father's middle name."

Una smiled. "No, Theophilus is a pretty awful name."

"Then what is it?"

"You said, 'I bet you're glad you weren't a boy.' "

Julien looked at her with confusion. "Well, aren't you? Aside from the middle name thing, would your life be any different if you had been a boy?"

Una snorted. "It would have been totally different!" But how could she explain her father's lack of attention to someone whose father lived and breathed for his well-being?

Julien shook his head. "But you'd still live in the Official Residence. You'd still have people waiting on you. You'd still have all the food you could ever want. You'd still have feather beds and leather boots and as many cucumbers as you could eat every day."

Una could sense his frustration. "You only see the things that you don't have when you look into someone else's life, not the things that you have."

"What do you mean? I've got nothing," he said earnestly.

"You have a father whose love was so strong that it literally brought me to the window of his jail."

Julien was confused. "But your father—"

Una interrupted. "I'm not a boy. Did you notice as I was

listing the generations that they were all men? Not a single woman there. And yet, did these men sprout from thin air? Where are their mothers? Their sisters? Their wives? Forgotten. That's where. It's as if they didn't exist. Only the men count in the histories. Only the men are remembered. Only the boys' births are celebrated."

Julien grew silent, thinking this through. He thought all along the pebble pathway toward the trees. As he ducked under branches heading toward a shortcut that he frequently used, he began to wonder. The more they walked, the bigger his question grew until he couldn't contain it any longer.

"If you think your life would have been so different as a boy, why don't you show your father that you're better?"

"Better than a boy?"

"Just better. That it doesn't matter if you were a girl or a boy."

Una felt a flicker of annoyance. What did he know about her father? But then her annoyance fizzled. Julien had a father—one who loved him the way her mother had loved her. Of that, she was sure.

Maybe he was right. Maybe she had never given her father a chance to know her value.

Maybe she needed to show her father she *was* better.

She would have to think about this.

Julien glanced back at her. "How about if I tell you one of the stories I know?"

38

The Marauders

Long after honest men were awake and about their business, the marauders still snored. Cassius, Brutus, and the other men had been up late the night before, making plans to find the missing Una. And so it was that they slept deep into the morning, leaving the weasel-voiced man as guard.

It was into this band of snorers that Florian stumbled. Unfortunately for Florian, he missed seeing Julien and Una's shortcut because he was dealing with the muck from the dumped cart. He assumed, wrongly, that they wouldn't get far and that he would be able to catch up with them on the mountain.

"Sharp as a tack, old Florian! Clever as ever," he said to himself. "You don't smell so good, though. Doesn't matter. You'll smell better once you have the silva flower."

Una gratefully said yes.

And so as they walked, Julien told her a story a woman who saved her family from their enemies with a wit and a red thread.

When Florian came hiking up the pathway, he was immediately taken. The Weasel caught him, and rather than driving him off, he marched the cowering man into their camp at the opposite end of his sword, certain of receiving praise from their leader, as his fellow marauder had the previous day when he captured Julien.

He thought wrong.

"Brutus!" the Weasel cried out. "Brutus, wake up!" Having been nearly delirious from lack of sleep, the man's reasoning skills were either not at their sharpest or else no one had ever taught him about waking a sleeping tiger.

Brutus shot out of his tent, alert but bleary-eyed, knife in hand. Cassius gave a whiffley snort, then he, too, leaped up, wide awake. At least, they both seemed awake. The truth was that they had only been asleep for two hours, so they, too, felt the effects from lack of sleep.

"Brutus, I caught a trespasser!"

Brutus blinked once, then repeated the weasel guard's words. "You caught a trespasser?"

The guard was certain of forthcoming praise and honor since they had spent the previous day searching for the girl. Having been unsuccessful in finding her, the Weasel figured the next best thing was to return to searching for the silva flower. He nearly shivered with anticipation. This wasn't the girl, but undoubtedly this one would help them track down the flower since the only people out here were collectors and marauders.

Florian, standing at sword point, quaked with fear. Here before him was the very man—Brutus—to whom Florian owed so much money. He slumped down and turned his face away, so that Brutus wouldn't recognize him.

Luck (and muck) was with Florian, for Brutus didn't even bother to look at him, stinking and splashed with manure as he was.

"You idiot!" Brutus blew up. "You've brought an outsider into our camp who will now require a guard and food."

The guard stopped his excited prancing. "But he must be looking for the silva flower like the boy, and I thought—"

Brutus interrupted him. "Do not think. You are not here to think. You are here to guard. Now, since you were so anxious to capture him, you will guard him *and* you will share your food with him." Brutus was perhaps harsher than he normally would have been, but he was not a morning person.

"Tie him up," Brutus said with resignation. "Put him by that tree and guard him until we figure out what to do with him."

Brutus was determined to get more sleep. He returned to his tent and settled in, a soft pillow at his head. He breathed deeply and began visualizing gold coins falling into a leather sack. One gold coin. *Clink.* Two gold coins. *Clink.* Three gold coins. *Clink.* Coin after coin dropped into his imaginary leather sack. Before long, he was rolling in them. He was floating upon a sea of gold coins. He was tossing them up in the air to rain down around him.

While he slept, the weasel-voiced marauder was joined by Cassius, who did not have the same ability to put himself to sleep by counting gold coins. "Let's tie him up," he said.

"I'll get some rope. You guard him."

While the weasel marauder headed to the saddlebags by the horses, Cassius unsheathed his sword and stood there, studying it.

Florian didn't feel particularly safe in the company of a man wearing the guard's uniform of the Magister Populi, especially not one who had his sword outstretched. Still, opportunities rarely come twice so he decided to take a chance.

Speaking quickly and in a low voice, he said, "Will you release me? I have business to attend to, though it has nothing to do with treasure. It is nothing that would interest any of you, especially not Brutus."

The man rubbed at a spot on his sword. "How might you know what interests us and what doesn't?"

Florian, utterly ignorant that these marauders had spent the past day searching for Una, said, "I am seeking a boy and a girl. They have something that I need."

"Ah!" The man nodded. "I see."

By that time, the Weasel was back with some rope to tie up Florian. Cassius sheathed his sword. They bound his wrists, then his ankles. Florian knew better than to fight them with that sword in such close proximity, even if it was sheathed, but he didn't look forward to the time when he would come face-to-face with Brutus.

"I'll take over the guard now. You can get some sleep," Cassius said.

The Weasel gratefully sank down next to a tree and was soon snoring softly like the others.

Cassius eyed his prisoner. He sensed that the man's intelligence was as lacking as that of the Weasel's. An idea began to take shape in his head.

Florian sniffed, then said, "Surely a child would be of no interest for your lot."

"Surely. However, as it happens, I, myself, am looking for a young lady."

"A wife?"

Cassius shook his head. "No. I don't have the desire for a family yet."

He pulled out a shorter knife and walked toward Florian.

"I suppose not, as one of the Magister Populi's guards." Florian edged back as the knife came closer.

"As one of the Magister Populi's *former* guards," Cassius corrected.

Sweat rolled down Florian's face as he stared at the knife.

Then Cassius said, "Your hands?"

Florian lifted his bindings with a sigh of relief, and the man began cutting through the rope. When he finished, Florian flexed his wrists, rotating them as if to celebrate their newly gained freedom, even though he had been bound for mere minutes. "Thank you. I'm very grateful."

The man nodded, then began working on Florian's ankles. "What's your name?"

Florian hesitated. If he told him his name, it might get back to Brutus. "It's . . . Almus."

Cassius finished cutting through the final cord. "Almus. I am Cassius."

"I am in your debt, Cassius." Florian rubbed his ankles where the cords had cut into his skin.

"Yes." Cassius chuckled. "You are."

"I've never known someone like you to be unselfishly generous."

"Someone like me?" Cassius questioned.

"Perhaps I misjudge you because of the company you keep? Your comrades seem rather . . . rough."

"They're not my comrades."

"Oh?"

"No." Cassius sheathed his knife. "Some of them are my brothers."

Florian twitched at this knowledge. "I'll be off then."

"Not quite so fast."

"What is it that you want?" Florian asked, certain now that his freedom was not given from any innate good will. It would cost him something.

Cassius smiled and said, "I'd be very glad of your company. You said you were looking for a boy. Wouldn't it be funny if the boy you are looking for and the girl I'm looking for were traveling together?"

Taken by surprise, Florian tried to cover his astonishment by pulling a flake of muck off his breeches.

"Funny, indeed." But Florian didn't laugh. He suspected that the girl this man was looking for was the same one he saw—a girl he called Opportunity who was dressed in expensive linen and polished leather boots—and he didn't want to give up the fancy baubles that she undoubtedly had.

But it seemed he had no choice.

39

Baba

Baba's newfound health took him out of the grounds of the Official Residence, through the city, past the gates, across the fields, and toward the mountain and the short-cut he knew Julien would use. He took a deep breath, filling his lungs, feeling his energy all the way down into his toes. How marvelous that soup had been! He studied the glorious sky, the steadfast trees, the abundant plants at his feet. What a wonderful day for collecting. He hadn't felt this alive in years.

It was while hiking that path that his vigor began to flag. Suddenly, he didn't feel quite so strong anymore. His lungs didn't feel quite so open, and he coughed. Then coughed again. His limbs grew haggard. More than anything, he wanted to sleep.

This, however, was not a good place to sleep. The pathway was rocky and rather damp. But farther ahead, there was a break in the trees with a nice sunny meadow of wildflowers. If he could make it that far, then he could rest.

40

Una and Julien

It was nearly midday. Julien and Una had reached a meadow of wildflowers that had been recently trampled.

"What a waste," Julien said, ever pragmatic. "What do you think happened here?"

Una pointed to a hoof print. "The marauders. I bet this was the source of the scent that I smelled in the tree."

"You think?" Julien lifted a broken stem of chamomile, showing Una the round yellow center ringed by white petals. "Did you have chamomile at the Official Residence?" He pulled off the flower head, leaving some buds lower down to blossom, and tucked it into a small sack tied to his waist.

"Yes, there was quite a lot of it in the garden."

"I was once in the garden at the Official Residence," Julien said as they walked through the field.

"You were?"

Julien nodded. "I was about five, I think. It was the year when great swarms of locusts blew in from the west. They made the sky go dark."

Una shuddered.

"Baba and I had been in the market. He was inside one of the shops selling our botanicals, but I was waiting outside the door. The guards grabbed dozens of people—including me—and told us to go fight the locusts. They herded us into the maze of the Official Residence until we came to the gardens. They told us to kill as many locusts as we could before they decimated the plants."

"I remember that." Una twirled a broken stem in her hands. "It was right before a feast that my father had arranged. Dozens of guests from all over the land were staying at the Official Residence. I heard rumors that there was going to be a dessert made of spun sugar that was a miniature rendering of the Official Residence, its gardens, and the inhabitants."

Julien's eyes widened. "Really?"

"Yes. I desperately wanted to see it."

Julien heard a note of disappointment in her voice. "Did you see it?"

Una dropped the broken stem on the ground. "No. The locusts came just before the feast. The sugar model was destroyed when the cooks tried to beat off the ones that had snuck through cracks into the kitchen. All that was left were shards of hardened sugar and a big sticky mess speckled with locust legs and antennae—or so I was told by Ovid. It was the greatest disappointment of my life up to that point."

The two continued walking at a steady pace. The coarse grasses were dotted with trees, then low bushes, then mossy rocks, all fed by the mountain streams. There was a huge patch of rockrose somewhere nearby, but Julien couldn't remember the exact location.

Years had passed since he and Baba had come this way because the process of gathering rockrose was long and arduous. It wasn't just picking flowers or digging up roots. It involved beating the stalks and flowers with a net to capture the sticky resin, then boiling the net in water until the resin floated to the top. Harvesting was best done in the hot months, which was, of course, when so many other plants and resins needed to be harvested. Baba said he didn't have the luxury of harvesting the rockrose. It took too much effort and time, and while the payoff was great, if a single step went wrong, their livelihood was at stake. They needed to eat. So they rarely gathered rockrose.

Julien thought for a minute, tracing their route in his mind to the patch of fertile ground where Baba said the angel's wings should be. "This way," he said, pointing north toward a barely visible path flanked by scrubby bushes. They had to cross the creek first.

He found a shallow spot where they could cross, then returned their conversation to the garden and locusts. "That's too bad you never got to see the miniature of the Official Residence."

Una nodded. "But at least we had the gardens. That's the one thing I miss about the Residence. Did you get to see any of the gardens?" Una asked. "I mean, aside from the locusts."

Julien began hopping from stone to stone to stone across the creek. "I didn't see much, but I remember these bushes that looked like living dragons." He lost his balance and nearly toppled into the water. "It was the most horrifying thing I've ever heard."

"Heard?" Una followed after him, leaping from one stone to the next.

Julien looked like he hadn't meant to say that. "I mean, seen."

But Una wouldn't let it go so easily. "No, you said heard." She landed next to him on the other edge of the creek.

"Well, the locusts were humming. I was so scared that I ran to the corner of the wall and curled up with my fingers in my ears." He hitched the sack from Ovid higher on his shoulders. "They drowned out the sounds of the leaves unfurling and the sap flowing in the trees."

Una gazed at him strangely. "You can hear the leaves unfurling?"

Julien looked embarrassed, and yet defiant at the same time. "Yes. I hear things that nobody else seems to hear. It's the only reason I'm any good at collecting botanicals."

"I've never heard of anyone who could do that," Una said.

"But it's nothing to be ashamed of. On the contrary, it seems like a gift. I pick up scents in a deeper way than anyone I know, but it's always been a good thing. That's why my mother's scent is so special."

Julien fiddled with the strap on the pack. "I haven't ever told anyone about it before. Not even Baba."

"I won't say anything if you don't want me to."

Julien shrugged and changed the subject. "Baba said the angel's wings should be on this side of the creek. The plants grow about this high." He held his hand out at his knees. "He also said there might be white flowers on them."

"I should be able to smell them before I see them, anyway. If it's the right scent, that is." Una made her way to a grassy spot. "You should be able to hear it, too, shouldn't you? Or doesn't it work that way?"

"It would if I was familiar with angel's wings, but since I've never come across them, I don't know exactly what to listen for."

"Hey!" Una cried out. She pointed toward a group of plants covered with clusters of white flowers, standing about thirty feet off their path to the left.

Julien caught sight of them and quickened his pace. He didn't recognize the plant, and so by process of elimination, he hoped they were angel's wings. When he reached the flowers, he examined their leaves. They were exactly as he would imagine angel's wings to look—feathery and long, curved at the top coming down to a point at their tip. "Yes! This must be it!" He turned to Una in jubilation, expecting her to be equally joyful.

Una was crestfallen. Up close, these flowers looked exactly like the flowers that grew outside her garden's window—the ones that Cassius saved from the caterpillar. Disappointment filtered through the air surrounding her, and her lips turned down in a frown.

So intent was he on finding the angel's wings, Julien had forgotten they were in search of a scent, not a plant. And clearly, the angel's wings weren't the scent she was looking for. "This isn't right," he said, knowing it to be so.

Una pulled a flower to her face and inhaled deeply, her disappointment growing. "No. And what's worse, we have these flowers at the Official Residence. The smell is close. But it's not quite right." It might have been her mother's favorite scent, but it wasn't *her* scent. Her mother was gone, her scent was gone, and all that remained was a wisp of memory that was slowly fading.

41

Cassius and Florian

Cassius was convinced that he would have a better chance to reclaim Una on his own rather than with all the other marauders, considering the ruckus they had created yesterday. Florian might prove to be an asset, though, as he seemed to know the mountain. He also seemed to know where the children were going.

"Let's take a walk," Cassius said.

Florian gulped. Taking a walk had never sounded so ominous.

They headed away from the marauders' camp with as much stealth as they could muster, for neither of them wished to awaken the others.

Cassius was a silent and rather menacing travel companion. He didn't say much, even though Florian pestered him with questions to prevent Cassius from questioning *him* about the boy he was tracking. When he ran out of things to say, Florian said, "Perhaps we should part ways. I feel as if my company is wearisome to you." It was quite the opposite really, but Florian was clever enough not to say so.

Amused, Cassius said, "Indeed not. In fact, I believe we shall travel together until we reach our prize."

Florian didn't like the sound of that. Eventually, he stopped speaking, and kept his thoughts to himself, trying to come up with a plan to ditch Cassius so he could find the two children himself. Except Cassius stuck to him like glue. So he turned his thoughts to the children.

When he had last seen them, they were heading toward the northwest. He had assumed that meant they were going to the path up the mountain, which was why he had followed that path. But he had neither seen nor heard any sign of them and then he had been captured by the marauders, so perhaps they had gone in a different direction? Perhaps if he went farther up the mountain, toward the meadow, he could find them? Maybe he could shake Cassius there, too. "You're sharp as a tack, Florian," he told himself. "You'll lose him soon enough."

Florian knew the lay of the land, even if he hadn't been here in years. His time spent collecting for his father left the paths engraved in his mind. At least, that's what he told himself. Unfortunately for him, he hadn't taken into consideration that the paths he knew had been changed by time and weather. Trees had fallen, flooding had altered the streams, and leaves and people and animals had changed the routes enough to leave Florian in a constant state of uncertainty. But he kept giving himself pep talks to keep up his spirits.

The two passed through a churned-up meadow, and Florian wondered if the silva flower was somewhere in all the mess. He decided to come back later once he escaped Cassius. "Sharp as a tack," he whispered.

At the edge of the meadow, he saw a pair of footprints: small, dainty boot prints to be exact, and he knew he was on the right trail. His clever eyes spotted the evidence leading to the path they had taken, and he hurried along after them, with Cassius close behind.

What Florian didn't know was that there was a small hole in the ground not far from him. And that hole held a nest. It was a hornet's nest, where hundreds of hornets were getting stirred up by the earthquake of steps that was happening above them. Stingers out, they flew to war.

42

Una and Julien

Julien walked to a ledge looking out over the valley. He sat down and let his legs swing over the edge. Una sat next to him and gazed across the landscape. Julien had no idea what to do now. Baba would not be satisfied if he hadn't helped Una get her mother's scent. But chasing a scent was akin to chasing the wind—for Julien at least.

Una dug her fingers into the grass surrounding her. "I thought that finding my mother's scent would seal her in my memory. Then I convinced myself that finding my mother's family would be even better—that it would bring me what I was missing. But that's not possible. Not with Cassius being one of those marauders." She plucked a blade of grass, then held it to her face, breathing in its greenness. "I still wish I could find my mother's scent, but she's gone, and she's not coming back."

Julien patted her shoulder awkwardly. He didn't know what to do with her grief. If only the angel's wings had been right, they might be celebrating. Instead, Una seemed hollow, and that was almost frightening to him.

"We should go back to your father," Una said, her voice sounding very small.

"Baba would be unhappy that we didn't keep looking." Julien sifted through his memories of all the plants he and Baba had collected over the years. There was very little that wasn't common. There was very little that Una wouldn't have had access to in her gardens at the Official Residence. It was almost comical thinking that he, the boy who couldn't smell, would be able to find a particular scent and present it to this girl. But he would try. "Do you know calamus, sometimes called sweet flag? What about styrax?"

Una shook her head. "I know neither."

"We're close to both. We should be able to find some styrax along the higher slopes. There might be some sweet flag by the creek. We could try the rockrose, too. We're not far from that. One of those might have the scent you're looking for."

"Maybe."

"Don't give up yet."

Una smiled at Julien. "Thanks. I won't."

"First, let's eat. Ovid sent all this food, and I'd rather be carrying it in my stomach than on my back."

43

Baba

Baba valiantly pressed onward, even though he was pale and sweat dripped down the sides of his face. He had reached the edge of the meadow where he had planned to rest, but the masses of wildflowers lay broken and scattered. This had been one of his favorite places to go collecting and it was ruined now. That filled him with sorrow.

This whole trip filled him with sorrow. Why had he left the Official Residence? Why had he left his room? Ovid was sure to be worried by now, he thought as he lowered himself onto a fallen tree trunk. He was worried, too.

At his feet, he saw a chamomile plant, leaves undisturbed but with empty stems, as if someone had neatly plucked flowers from the top of the plant. At the bottom, a few buds were left to keep the plant alive and healthy. This was the way that he'd taught Julien to gather chamomile. They couldn't be too far ahead of him.

Baba would lie down here for some rest, and when he had regained a bit of strength, he would set out once more, following the trail that Julien undoubtedly left.

44

Una and Julien

Julien opened the pack from Ovid and pulled out the cucumbers, the flask of loganberry juice, and the walnuts. To be honest, even though he was disappointed at their quest, he was excited at the prospect of such a feast. It wasn't bread or foraged greens like he usually had, but a crisp cucumber! And nuts that had already been shelled! Even the loganberry juice was new for him and he longed to taste it.

He listened to the trickle of water in the distance. "We can backtrack toward the creek and search for the sweet flag there since it grows in wet areas. We'll look for rushes."

"Rushes?"

"Like long grasses. They have bright green leaves like swords and a long flower that's about the size of a finger."

Una brushed off her hands as best as she could, wiping the

dirt on the grass until they were nearly clean. She showed them to Julien. "Is that clean enough?"

He laughed and showed her his hands. They weren't much better.

When Una sat down, the smallest whiff of a scent came to her on the breeze. It was an unfamiliar smell—an animal scent of corruption and decay, more sour than even the rubbish pit back at the Official Residence. The scent was so putrid that she couldn't help but groan. "What is that?"

Julien sat up quickly, listening, then grabbed her hand, pulled her to standing, and began running. The putrid scent seemed to be all around Una: in the air she breathed, in the ground below her, in the leaves of the plants she trod on. It confused her, this scent. It made her mind go blank. All she could do was keep moving, holding onto Julien's hand, but the scent became stronger as if she were getting closer to it.

Julien pushed her toward a large tree. "Up!"

She leaped up to grab the lowest branch and began climbing, with Julien scaling the tree behind her.

Down below, a large wild sow with five piglets trotted into the clearing. The piglets went straight for the food that Julien had so nicely laid out. The sow snuffled Una's sack, then Ovid's sack. There were interesting things there. Things she wanted to eat. Things that would make her piglets strong.

Julien called out, making as much noise as he could, shaking the branches of the tree, and shouting, but to no avail. Not when there was a feast for the taking. He groaned as the piglets tore into the cucumbers, chewing and slurping until not a single bit was left. They crunched their way through the nuts, then they turned to the rest of the food, pawing out the raisins, the dried pears, and the pistachios, quickly demolishing them.

The two shouted and shook branches from their place of safety in the tree, but the animals would not be scared away. There were no chestnuts to throw this time, and neither had grabbed anything when they ran. They didn't dare climb down the tree, for wild pigs could be quite dangerous, especially when there were piglets involved.

When Ovid's feast was gone, the piglets broke open Una's sack.

"No!" she shouted. "That's not yours!"

The sow narrowed her eyes at them, wondering how much of a threat these creatures posed to her piglets. She could easily send her 250 pounds against the tree. She decided it was not a threat. The piglets paid no attention to Una.

Una watched them make a mess of her belongings. Her scent collection was rooted out and they broke open the box. Shards of glass scattered everywhere as they pawed through the edible contents: the rose hips, the lavender buds, the ambergris, the musk, the citron, the anise. They even snuffled through the vial of civet.

Their muddy prints marred the area. It seemed as if

everything that had been in a vial was now broken and destroyed—or eaten. And all Una and Julien could do was watch.

When the mama sow found nothing more to eat, she decided it was time to look for greener pastures. She grunted at the piglets and did an about-face, snuffling her way toward a new place that smelled more promising.

After the sow and piglets had gone, Una and Julien climbed down the tree, completely dejected. Nothing had been spared.

45

Una and Julien

Julien was heartsick. Why hadn't he grabbed the pack before he ran? Then they would at least have some food. But now they had nothing. "Do you want to go back?" he asked Una. "We don't have any food now. I mean, nothing that you're used to. I can find us something edible, but it won't be cucumbers or dried fruit."

Una stood with her hands on her hips. "Well, I don't want to go back when you've convinced me there still might be some hope."

"All right. Is there anything here worth saving?" Julien looked at their scattered belongings.

"Not much." Una began gathering her gardening tools and anything else that looked remotely salvageable. One vial from her scent collection lay unbroken. It was the hartshorn.

Julien brushed off the sack that Ovid had packed the food

in. It was empty, but for the flask of loganberry juice, along with the flint and steel and the small pot for boiling water.

They both stood with their regret for a moment before Julien directed them toward the creek.

"Good thing we're going to the creek first," he said. "If we drink a lot of water, it will fill our stomachs. I sometimes do that when we haven't got much."

Una turned to look at him, stricken to think that he didn't always have enough to eat. She followed him back to the creek, quiet with these thoughts.

In minutes they had reached their destination. Julien scanned the area, listening for the sound of sweet flag while Una knelt down, scooping water into her mouth in big gulps. Not hearing any sweet flag, Julien joined Una at the brook and drank his fill.

Her thirst satisfied, Una sat back. Drops of water trickled down her front. "Should we walk along the creek to look?"

Julien nodded, then took a big step up onto one of the rocks at the edge of the brook. "I remember the first time Baba brought me here, this part of the journey seemed so endless to me. I was much smaller then. I climbed until I couldn't move my legs anymore. Then Baba lifted me high onto his shoulders, and we continued that way. I had a grand view. It seems strange to be up here without Baba."

"You miss him, don't you?"

Julien looked at her strangely. "Of course I miss him. He's my world."

"You know you're his world, too."

"I suppose."

"No, really. You are," Una said. "That's why I came after you originally—when I got you out of the tent."

"What do you mean?"

"The scent of your father's love for you was so strong, it made me miss my mother so much, and it pulled me to the jail. I couldn't stand by when someone else was feeling the same misery, especially if there was something that I could do to reunite you."

"I wish I could have sensed that."

"You couldn't? The air was thick with it."

Julien shrugged. "I can't smell."

"You can't smell?"

"No. Or at least, I don't think I can. To be honest, I'm not sure what smell is."

"You can't smell anything?"

Julien shook his head. "Not a thing."

Una wasn't sure she believed him. "You can hear leaves unfurl, but you can't smell?"

"I've never been able to smell. I didn't know what Baba was talking about when he would ask me to smell something. I could sort things for him because I knew what they sounded like. I knew what they looked like. But I don't know smell."

"Is there anything else I should know about you?"

Julien laughed. "No. That's it, really."

"You know what I really want to know?"

"What?"

"What you're going to find for us to eat tonight!" Una laughed, then linked her arm in his and they set off along the creek.

46

Florian

Florian ran with abandon, not caring whether Cassius followed him or not. Not caring whether he found the children or not. Not caring where he ended up as long as it was far away from those stinging hornets.

And he did end up far away—far away from hornets, children, and Cassius. In fact, he was so far that he didn't know where he was. Things only got worse for Florian, because the path beneath his feet grew steep and rocky. He had to scrabble, using his hands to help pull himself up, which was not easy, considering they were covered in hornet stings.

When Florian found a slight ledge, he decided to pause there to catch his breath. He took stock of his stings—he thought there were about fifty, but he couldn't be sure, as one hornet seemed to have crawled up his sleeve and stung him multiple times. The stings were starting to swell, and Florian had never been in such misery.

He sat on the ledge and looked out into the distance, trying to catch sight of the two children. He saw nothing but trees and grass, and knowing that Cassius could be right behind him, the children could be right in front of him, and the hornets could be anywhere, he decided it would be in his best interest to keep moving.

Florian picked up a stick, ready to start swinging if he needed to, and left so quickly that he never noticed the band of men wearing the uniform of the Magister Populi's guards moving in his direction across the field in the distance.

47

Una and Julien

It wasn't long before Una and Julien came to a marshy area where the rushes grew thick. Julien found a stand of sweet flag plants, and pulled one up from its roots. He folded a leaf to break open its scent and held it out to Una.

She closed her eyes and inhaled deeply. "It's lovely—kind of spicy. Quite nice, actually."

"But it's not right."

"No. Not right."

"On to styrax then?" Julien's words were brave, but his worry grew.

"On to styrax," Una repeated. But before she left, she wrapped the sweet flag and put it in the pack alongside her vial of hartshorn.

The path that Una and Julien followed was difficult as it rose quickly. They didn't speak as they pulled themselves up the steep slope, holding on to the roots and gnarled stems of the bushes.

Julien heard Una scrabbling up the path behind him, and he slowed their pace. "Not too much farther before the land evens out. We should start seeing the styrax soon." He paused when they reached the top of the challenging ascent.

"What does styrax look like?" Una panted, trying to catch her breath.

"It would be easier for me to tell you what it sounds like, but since that won't help you, all I can say is that it's a type of bush. It has pink or white flowers early in the season, but there won't be any now." He paused, then said, "Una, what do you want to do if it's not the right scent?"

Una hesitated. "Did you want to go back? Are you worried about your father?"

Julien's face grew apologetic. "I *am* worried, but Baba won't be happy until we've exhausted all possibilities."

"I don't think there are many more possibilities, anyway. Try not to worry," Una said. "I know that's easy for me to say when it's not my father, but Ovid has nursed me through many sicknesses. He'll take good care of him."

Julien nodded. They gazed out at the whole valley below. Una studied the city in the distance, the stone and brick architecture, the streets, the market. How different it appeared from up here. How different it seemed from outside the Official Residence.

Julien pointed to the southwest corner of the city. "That's where we live."

Una saw a mass of small stone huts crowded together and tried to imagine the noise, the people, the smell, but all she saw in her mind were the corridors in the Official Residence where her mother had walked, wide and breezy, quiet and fresh. She couldn't imagine life outside of the Official Residence, because she had never *been* outside of the Official Residence. She wondered if her father had ever seen the whole city this way.

Julien pointed to a more central spot. "And that open area there is the market where we sell our botanicals every day."

Una tried to picture the market, but again, she found she could not. She had no idea if there were stalls or portable carts or shop fronts. Was there food? Fruits and vegetables? Bread? What about household things, like thread or spoons? Could a person get anything she wanted there? She doubted that her father had ever been to the market.

Julien motioned farther east. "There's the Official Residence. See the walls? Beyond those trees are the gardens."

On the other side of those walls, her father was governing this land, and her stepmother was settling into her roles of Magistrix and mother. Inside the Official Residence, her two younger brothers knew nothing of this world outside either, just as she hadn't until recently.

This view—this reality—was an abrupt education. She thought of Vita and her spicy soup and of Ovid with his smell of sweet syrup. How many other people were there in the city like them? Like Julien and his father? How many people didn't have enough to eat? How many people lived in uncertainty every day, worried about their survival?

"Everything is so clear from up here," she said slowly. And Una did see clearly. She saw what she had: a home, a father, a stepmother, two younger brothers, Ovid, and all the privileges that came with that life. Food, clothing, education, space, anything that she could need or want. It was not perfect, but it was far more than anyone else in Antiquitilla had. And yet, she had spent so much time and effort seeking something that she could never obtain. Chasing a scent was like trying to gather water that just slipped through your fingers. There was nothing to hold on to. Maybe what she sought didn't even exist, except in her mind.

Her mother was gone. She would always love and miss her, but what about her life now? Shouldn't she appreciate what she had? Shouldn't she do something positive with her privileges? What must Julien think of her and her quest when he didn't have enough to eat despite working day in and day out at his father's side? How indulged and self-centered she must seem to him. How indulged and self-centered she seemed to herself.

Una needed to be *better*, like Julien had said. She needed to step into who she was meant to become.

She turned to Julien. "You're right."

"About styrax?"

"No, about showing my father that I'm better."

That was not what Julien had been expecting her to say.

"You've helped me understand a lot," she said.

"Like what? The plant life outside the city?"

"No. My mother's gone. The one person I have left is my father. I want him to see me for who I am, the way your father sees you for who you are. I want him to see that I'm capable of doing good things, and that I want to *do* good things. But I don't think I can do that until my father sees me as competent, and I don't think my father will see me as competent unless I can do something meaningful. That would show I'm capable— and maybe even more. Maybe then he'll believe I'm worth his time."

Julien smiled. "Do you have something in mind?"

"I was thinking," Una said slowly, "about finding the silva flower. Do you think that's dumb?"

"Not at all. But we might need to get Baba's help finding it . . . and hope no one beats us there."

Una waved a blade of grass back and forth. "I know this is not going to be easy, and I know that we might not find the flower, but I also know that you and I both have abilities that set us apart. If you put them together, I think we have a greater chance at finding the silva flower than anyone else out there. What you hear and what I smell gives us an advantage. I think we need to trust that and take a chance."

Julien nodded slowly. "All right. I'll look for as long as you want."

"You'll do this with me? Really?"

"Of course. Baba told me before that the silva plants would be in the bog, which is over that way." He pointed toward a rocky outcropping in the distance. "It's possible we'll even find some styrax on the way."

"We're in this together—if we find the silva, I want you to get the reward."

Julien smiled. "I promise I won't turn it down." He took note of the various plants around him. Wild onion, hyssop, grass, mint, wood sorrel. He pulled up some wood sorrel and passed it to Una. "Here. Have some. If we're going to stay out for a while, we need to eat."

"What is it?"

He told her. "It's not bad. A bit sour, but it's better than nothing."

Una took some and began chewing. She made a face. "It *is* sour. But like you said, we should eat." She chewed more and swallowed, then looked at the sky. "We should keep going. Night will be coming soon."

"Have you ever been away from home at night?"

Una shook her head. "Other than last night, no."

"I've spent many nights up here with Baba when we've been gathering. We can find a hollow tree or make some kind of shelter if you'd like."

"Thank you," she said. "Really."

Julien smiled. "You helped me get Baba out of jail. It's the least I can do."

48

Una and Julien

Julien walked on before speaking again. "I always thought that it was bad luck that shaped my life. Bad luck that made my mother die. Bad luck that Baba got sick. Bad luck that we are poor. And maybe it is, but did bad luck put you where you are? Is it the same bad luck that puts anyone anywhere? Is it luck or is it chance? Most people would say that being born the daughter of the Magister Populi is good luck. But is it really? Is it worse to be born the daughter of the Magister and feel unwanted or to be born the son of a pauper but have as much love as you want? I'm beginning to think it's all one and the same. I get one thing, you get another. But we both have our own struggles."

Una considered that. "I suppose you're right. We all struggle in different ways. Maybe that's the nature of life, and we have to climb our way out of our challenges, whatever they are."

"And those challenges are always different based on our circumstances."

Una sidestepped a fallen branch. "But what we do with those circumstances, or what choices we make, decides our future. Maybe happiness comes from our choices, not from our circumstances."

Julien turned to her. "Right—like you could have simply decided to live your life at the Official Residence, but instead you chose to look for your mother's past. You chose to seek out my father in the prison. You chose to free me from the marauders. You're on a pathway built from your choices."

Una smiled. "And I'm happier now than I used to be. What about you? You didn't have to come back looking for me—you could have stayed with your father. You could have returned home after we found the angel's wings or the sweet flag. Even now, you've insisted on staying to help me, even if it means you eat only wood sorrel for the next few days."

Julien laughed. "Wait until you see what we eat tomorrow."

Una laughed with him. "We might not know what the future brings, but I do hope it isn't just a field full of wood sorrel."

"I hope it isn't another wild sow with piglets looking for a second course!"

"I hope it isn't an uncle who wants to kidnap us—even if he does have meat cooking over a fire!"

"I hope it isn't a marauder who sounds like a weasel and puts a dirty rag in my mouth. To be honest, I'd rather have wood sorrel."

"Me, too. In fact, is there any more?"

Julien plucked another couple of leaves and handed them to Una.

As she ate, she felt more optimistic than she had in a long time. Perhaps it was having a friend for a companion. Perhaps they really would find the silva flower. "You said that the silva might be in the bog."

"That's what Baba thinks. But I've never been in the bog, so I couldn't say."

"Why not?"

"It's dangerous. The ground is waterlogged and you never know if you're going to step on solid ground or sink down to your knees in mud."

Una began to lose her optimism.

"But Baba also told me a few hints about the bog. He said to choose your steps slowly and carefully. I think that will help us know if a place is safe to walk or not."

"Did he say anything else?"

"He said to stay away from the dark areas and bright vivid green."

"I wonder why," Una said.

"I guess we'll see when we get there."

The two continued on, moving higher as they went.

"If you've never been to the bog, how do you know where it is?" Una asked.

Julien shrugged. "Because I know where everything else is. It was really the only place Baba didn't allow me to go. I don't think it's too much farther."

It wasn't. Within minutes they left the rocky path and before them lay a vast open area. Long grasses and small shrubs covered the land, but there were also elevated mounds surrounded by dark muddy areas.

Una wasn't sure what she expected, but this wasn't it.

Julien found a sturdy stick and picked it up. "There's probably enough light left to look around a bit, but I don't think we should go too far."

Seeing the stick, Una remembered Baba's instruction at the prison. She followed Julien's lead and found a stick also. "Well, at least I don't see any brilliant green."

"Yes, but I don't hear anything that might be a silva plant either."

"It can't be that easy or there wouldn't be a prize for finding one. We'll have to work together. You'll need to listen and I'll need to smell, and then we can combine that information."

"Maybe we should put together a shelter for tonight and get to know the bog from here first."

"Good idea," Una said. "That way you'll learn its regular sounds and I'll figure out its usual smells."

"Then if I hear something unusual or you smell something unusual, we can look for the silva plant there."

"We can narrow down what we learn until we find it."

It seemed like a foolproof plan, but Una and Julien didn't recognize quite how dangerous the bog really was.

49

Baba

Baba had rested for the bulk of the day in the meadow. It was only when he heard horses approaching and the voices of brash men that he decided to duck behind a bush. Baba had spent enough time in these parts to know that not everyone who came through the wilderness had honest intentions. Not everyone had a good heart. After all, somebody had churned up this meadow without a second thought. It might be the same men who approached now.

And in fact, it was.

"I don't want to hear another word from you!" one of them shouted over the sound of the horses.

"But—"

"The boy. The girl. You even let them take our breakfast right off the fire! You wake me up, you bring a prisoner into our camp, then you let him escape? He saw your face. He saw my face. There's going to be trouble and it's all because of you. It's undoubtedly your fault that Cassius is gone now, too."

"But—"

"Not a word!"

The marauder was not willing to be deterred from defending himself, though. "But I had nothing to do with the girl—that was all Cassius!"

"Don't you dare blame my brother!" the voice warned. "*You* were left to guard the camp, and *you* let them get away!"

Baba felt a chill go down his back. He didn't want to be on the wrong side of that voice.

"It's all because of *Cassius*," the sullen voice said.

Baba listened to this exchange, certain that these were the marauders who had captured Julien. If they were on the move, they might stumble upon Julien again. Baba needed to find him. No matter what it took, he had to make sure his son was safe.

When the marauders had moved on, Baba came out from behind the bush. And though evening approached and he was weak and pale, he continued walking.

50

Una and Julien

Una took out her clippers and began cutting some greenery to make a bed for herself. As she clipped, she breathed in the scents of the bog. The smell of decaying plant matter, earthiness, age. It was a warm smell that was almost comforting. In comparison, the greenery she cut for bedding smelled sharp and full of light. The two together gave her a feeling of transcendence and hope. She was certain she would sleep well tonight—even considering how far she was from her soft bed.

Una looked toward Julien, who was sitting on a rock with his eyes closed. As if he could sense her looking at him, he opened his eyes.

"Are you getting a feel for the plants in the bog?" she asked.

"Yes—they're mostly low and somber. I haven't heard anything unusual yet."

"Am I disturbing you, clipping these branches?"

"No. The sounds of the plants come in through my heart and my hands more than through my ears."

"Then I'll cut some for you, too, if you'd like?"

"Thank you. Have you smelled anything unusual?"

Una shook her head. "Not yet, but I'm still taking it all in."

Julien closed his eyes again and concentrated. A deep hum emerged from the moss, which was everywhere. Then there was a fluttery sound. He didn't know what that was yet, but it didn't sound like what he imagined a silva flower to sound like. It sounded more like rainberries than a rare flower.

He sat there pondering what a rare flower would sound like. Would it be like a horn announcing the approach of the Magister Populi? Staccato? Smooth? Sharp? He wasn't sure. But he needed to listen. So he sat quietly, separating out one sound from another, tracing a sound to its source.

Julien was concentrating so intensely that he hadn't noticed that Una had finished cutting branches for bedding. He didn't hear her step away from their solid, safe spot at the edge of the bog. His eyes were closed, so he didn't see a light flickering in the distance.

Una had seen it, though, and Vita's story had popped into her head. Foxfire and fox fairies and treasure. Vita said that foxfire marked a spot of treasure—treasure that could only be retrieved on St. John's Day. Was it St. John's Day? Una wasn't sure. She had lost track of time.

In the distance, the bluish light flickered. It wasn't too

far—about the span of her courtyard garden—and the ground leading up to it was the dark color of packed earth.

Una glanced at Julien, but he was concentrating so hard that she didn't want to disturb him. He had said to walk slowly and carefully in the bog. She could do that. He said to stay away from vivid green. There were only dull greens and dark browns here, so there was nothing to worry about.

She took a careful step toward the flickering light with her arms outstretched for balance and smelled the air. The warm earthy scent surrounded her. She took another step. If the silva flower was the treasure, she could get it on her own, then present it with Julien to her father. The air lost its sharp greenness as she left the edge of the bog and ventured inward. The thought of finding the silva flower made her feel triumphant, as if she already had the flower in hand.

It was then that a new scent wafted by her—a scent that was intense, not mellow like the rest of the bog. It was bright with a hint of caramel, and it snuck inside of her. It smelled vaguely familiar, like something she knew from when she was very young. It wasn't her mother's scent, but it reminded her, in some way, of her mother. Surprised, she turned in the direction of the scent.

Una's movement was too much for the fine web of water-logged peat beneath her. Her foot went through the surface, and she sank to her knee.

51

Una and Julien

The cold water seeping through her leather boot shocked Una and she gasped.

The sound broke Julien's concentration, and his eyes popped open. When he saw the danger Una was in, he cried out, "Don't move!"

But it was too late. Una was wiggling her foot back and forth, trying to release it from the grip of the bog. The harder she wiggled it, the deeper it went. Her other foot was beginning to sink now, too.

Julien looked around frantically for the stick he had found earlier. It was behind him, but when he picked it up, he realized it was far too short to reach Una from the safety of where he was standing. He'd never be able to pull her out.

"Una! Stop! You need to stop moving." His voice cut

through Una's panic, and she stopped struggling. She took a deep breath and closed her eyes, letting the scents of the bog drift up to her. First was the earthy peat. But underneath it was water. Lots and lots of water. It was as if her foot broke a hole in the peat that freed the smell of the water.

She looked over her shoulder and saw Julien pacing back and forth, trying to find a safe path to her. "We need to think our way out of this. Do you hear the water?"

"Yes. It's sloshy everywhere."

"How can we fight against water? A boat?"

"A bridge?"

"A dock?"

They both looked at the branches and leaves that Una had cut for their bedding.

"I don't know if that will be enough," Una said. "Can you find a place that doesn't sound so sloshy and work your way toward me?"

But Julien was already on the move, gathering an armful of branches and bringing them to the edge of the bog. He listened carefully, then laid one branch down on the surface of the bog, leading away from where she stood.

"I know it looks like I'm going in the wrong direction, but this way is safer." Julien laid another branch parallel to the first, then listened.

Another branch went down, then another. Slowly, a pathway grew, crisscrossing the surface of the bog, meandering because the depth of the peat was not consistent. He went back and forth, trip after trip, pausing to listen for the deepest sounds before he laid down more branches.

Una wished she could be working alongside Julien, rather than stuck where she was. She wished she hadn't been so foolish as to think she could come out here on her own. She regretted not thinking of laying down the branches earlier, as that would have prevented her from falling into her current predicament. Or even bringing a stick with her, the way Julien's father had recommended. Or remembering that Julien had warned her against both the bright green *and* the dark brown.

She watched Julien set branch after branch, sometimes shifting one an inch before putting his weight on it.

"I'm sorry," she said, hoping he wasn't angry.

"I'll be there as soon as I can, but I'm running out of branches."

"My clippers are on that rock if you need to cut more."

Julien nodded. "I'll try to be quick." He took the clippers and headed back into the trees.

The scents in the bog had been shifting while Julien had been moving around. Once he left, the smells settled and became more stable. Standing there alone in the darkening twilight, she found a multitude of scents hovering around her like music. First, the deep earthy brown smell undoubtedly rising up from the peat below her. Then a musky sad smell permeated through that, which she linked with the water saturating the peat.

Then a quick pitter-pat scent, which she discovered came from a small, clover-like plant growing near where she stood. How different these scents were from the ones she knew back home. As she stood there, an unusual scent curled around her, as if calling her by name. It was the scent that had caught her attention before, when her foot sank deep into the mud and peat. As she breathed it in, she found she could trace its direction. The scent seemed stronger now as the night grew, and she wished she could extract her foot so she could follow the scent to its origin.

Julien returned bearing an armload of branches. "Are you all right?"

Una's leg and back were slowly starting to cramp from standing off-balance. "I'm okay. I think I've found something rather interesting."

"Really?"

"Yes, but first things first. When you reach me, you can listen and see if you hear what I'm smelling."

"Deal." Julien returned to laying branches, crisscrossing his way to her.

As he drew closer, Una could sense what he was doing. One direction smelled stronger of earthy brown age, while another smelled of sad musk. She'd bet that the entire pathway of branches smelled of age, rather than musk.

The gap closed, and then he was beside her.

52

Una and Julien

Julien laid a raft of branches by Una to give them both a firm footing.

Una bent over to put her weight on the branches in an attempt to free her left foot—the one that wasn't so deeply encased in the mud. She slowly and carefully tried to ease it out.

"It doesn't seem like I'm making any progress," Una said.

"It's coming. I hear it," Julien said.

And sure enough, within a few moments the bog released her foot. She fell onto the branches, landing on her knee. She circled her ankle, grateful that it still worked.

"The next one is going to be harder," Julien said. "You might lose your boot because it's so deep in the mud."

Una shifted her weight on the mat to get better leverage. "As long as I don't lose my foot." She grunted, trying to heave her leg upward, but the mud sucked at her and it felt like she really was going to rip off her foot.

Julien listened closely to the ground near Una's leg, then took a stick and stabbed at the mud to release the suction. He tried to wiggle it around, but all he managed to do was lose his balance and fall backward.

Una stopped, panting at the effort. "I'm not sure this is going to work."

"It's got to work. How about if I grab under your arms and pull with you?"

"Let me rest for a minute."

The night had descended and the bog was now fully dark. Mist was rising, but Una could still see the same flickering light that had enticed her before.

"Do you see that?" she asked, pointing in its direction.

"What is it?"

"Vita told me a story about foxfire. That the light marks treasure left by fairies."

"Is that where you were going?"

"Yes," Una said, abashed. "I thought the silva plant might be there."

"Might be, but we can't see until we get you out. Want to give it another try?"

Una nodded. She grabbed the mat of sticks, and Julien grabbed Una under her arms. Together, they pulled with all their strength, and Una felt the mud surrounding her right leg shift. "Keep pulling!" she cried out, now lying almost completely horizontal, her left leg pushing against the frame of the branches. The mud and cold seeped into her clothes as her right leg began to rise.

"Almost there!"

Julien gave another great heave and Una hoisted herself free. They both fell on the mat, panting and covered in mud.

Una couldn't speak until the pounding of her heart quieted and her breath returned to normal. "Thank you," she finally said.

"You're welcome. But I'm guessing you're not going to want to sleep on these branches anymore, huh?"

Una could hear the smile in Julien's voice, and she would have laughed if she had the energy. She stayed there unmoving, letting the scents of the bog waft around her: the brown earthiness, the sad musk, the twittery clover. Once again, that unusual scent came to her, caramel and bright. "Do you hear anything, Julien?" she asked. "Anything unusual?"

"Yes. I've been listening and wondering if that's what you meant before."

"The scent is growing stronger. Do you think that might be the silva?"

"It could be."

"Do you want to try to find it now? I mean, I know it's dark, but we're both better versed at how this bog works. Besides, it seems like we can trust what you hear and what I smell better than we can trust what we see."

"We could continue building this pathway out to wherever it is."

"Exactly. We can always use some of the branches over again if we have to, but the scent is so strong here, I almost think another mat of branches might be enough."

In the moonlight, Julien nodded. "Let's do it."

53

Vita

Vita trundled back through the city streets heading toward the place she called home, muttering, "Soup of life has spice and lime, chiles, garlic, luck, and time." But as she pushed the cart, a thought occurred to her. Today's soup of life didn't have lime.

She forgot to put in the lime.

She forgot to put in the lime!

She thought back over all the people she had given soup to that day. The men and women. The children. Without the lime, the soup was not the same. It wouldn't have the strength necessary to make the sick well again. And that man in the Official Residence! The one who coughed so. Oh dear! She should do something, shouldn't she? How could she have made such a mistake? With something as important as soup, she needed to keep her wits about her at all times.

Well, she hadn't kept her wits about her. She had gotten distracted when that darling girl had surprised her that morning. Vita knew that as soon as she reached her home, she would find the lime juice ready and waiting.

Before she reached home, though, she was hailed.

"Grandmother," someone called out.

Vita lifted her head and saw a group of the Magister Populi's guards down the trail.

Her heart fluttered with fear. "Did . . . did you want soup?"

"No, Grandmother. We are searching for a girl."

"Oh?"

"Have you seen one?"

Vita studied the guards. She knew they must be searching for Una, but she had no desire to put Una's welfare into their hands. They looked like they had good intentions, but she could not be sure. Una, no doubt, knew what she was doing. At Una's age, she herself had taken on the care of her eight siblings.

"Have you seen one hereabouts?"

"I've seen many girls today. I am a soup-seller, after all. Who is it you seek? A thief, perhaps? A rabble-rouser?"

The man appeared scandalized. "No, indeed! We seek one of high birth who has gone missing."

"Is she traveling alone? Or with others?"

"I could not say."

Vita thought for a minute, as if reviewing all the girls she had met that day. Instead, she considered why a girl of high birth might run away, for certainly that was what had happened. Girls of high birth only ran away when the need was dire, for who would leave comfortable circumstances to throw their lot in with the unknown?

Vita looked at the man again. "That is very little information to go on. I cannot help you."

The man looked disappointed.

But the woman knew she could help Una. "Unless you want some soup? It is the last of this batch and I have no need for it. Perhaps you might do with a bit of refreshment?"

"That's very kind of you," the head guard said. He looked at the others, the hope showing on their faces. "We have been traveling all day with little food."

"Then let me get out some bowls." Vita made it appear as if she was hurrying to dish up the soup, but in reality, she moved back and forth without making much progress. Since it was too late to make a new batch of soup and deliver it to that nice man who was so sick, the least she could do would be to hold up these guards and give Una time to get away, for she had no doubt that Una did not want to be found.

Vita bustled back and forth, putting the pot over some coals she kept in a can. Except it was the wrong can. Then it was the wrong coals. Then the soup needed to heat. Then it needed to cool. Then she needed to wash the bowls before she could dish up the soup. Then the soup was too cool again and needed to reheat. By the time the soup was finally ready, the men had all fallen asleep, leaning against the trees.

54

Una and Julien

Una and Julien carefully got to their feet.

"Do you want to lay the next section?" Julien asked. "That way, we can see if we're both aiming for the same thing."

"Sure."

Julien backed up on the path of branches, giving Una space to determine the direction she wanted to go.

She breathed in deeply. She closed her eyes and tried to figure out the way that would blend the earthy brownness with the intense brightness, for that would be both the safest and the most direct way.

She turned from one direction to the next, and finally decided on a gentle turn to the right. She opened her eyes and pointed. "That way."

Julien nodded. "That's the exact way I would have chosen, too. I think we're on to something."

Una carefully set a branch on top of the bog. Julien grabbed another and laid it next to Una's. Then he closed his eyes and listened. When he opened them, he picked up another branch and laid it a bit more to the right. Una nodded.

They went back and forth like this, leading and following while extending the pathway until the scent and the sound were so strong and so loud that both of them were sure they must be right on top of their treasure.

"We're out of branches," Julien said.

"We shouldn't need any more. It should be right here."

They turned in a circle, trusting their senses, yet frustrated because they couldn't see what they wanted. As they stood there, a flash of bluish foxfire puffed nearby, lending a bit of light to the darkness.

It was in that light that they both saw a long stalk topped by a trumpeting red-and-white flower.

The silva flower.

55

Una and Julien

Una couldn't help herself. She whooped loudly. "We did it! Julien, we did it!"

Julien wanted to jump up and down, but he knew better after the ordeal of extracting Una from the mud, so he kept his enthusiasm limited to a big exhale of relief.

With the help of Una's gardening tools, they dug up the silva plant and carefully placed it in the sack from Ovid.

Now that they had found the flower and the excitement had ebbed, Una shivered with the cold. Her clothes were wet through with mud.

"I know it's late, but why don't we go back to the city?" Julien asked. "There's no reason to stay here, and you won't be any less comfortable heading back to the city than you would be staying here all night. Besides, the hike might even warm us up a bit."

Una nodded, her teeth chattering, and they set off, carefully retracing their steps through the wilderness. It took them most of the night, for the journey was long and rather treacherous in the dark. When they reached the stream, Una tried to wash off the mud, but the water was too cold, so she just cleaned her hands and dreamed about the hot bath and the hot chocolate and the hot soup that she would have at home.

At the ledge, they stopped, knowing that descending it in the dark would be too dangerous. There they slept for a short while, backs against each other in an attempt to stay warm.

When the sun began to peek above the horizon, Julien stirred. He heard Baba coughing. It was time to heat some water for his morning tea. He was so tired, though. Maybe just a minute more rest? His body ached and surely another minute wouldn't make a difference.

But then the cough came again.

Julien opened his eyes and recognized where he was. He also realized where Baba should be: at the Official Residence with Ovid.

And yet there was his cough.

Julien's movement woke Una. She yawned and stretched.

Julien was already on his feet. "Baba?" he called out. "Is that you?"

"Julien!" a weak voice came in reply.

Julien launched himself over the ledge and began descending in a half-controlled slide.

Una rushed over to see Julien go careening downward. She

grabbed her pack and the sack from Ovid and followed after him.

When she reached the bottom, Julien was leaning over a man—a man she knew must be Baba.

He looked just as Una expected—kind and intelligent, but also pale and sickly. The scent of his love for Julien whirled around them. But the scent was overlaid by something unhealthy.

"You must be Julien's father," she said. "I'm so glad that he was able to free you."

"With many thanks to you." The skin around Baba's eyes crinkled as he smiled. "We are so very grateful."

Una could smell Julien's worry for his father, just as she could smell Baba's love for his son. Julien tilted his head, as if listening intently.

"Baba, why aren't you with Ovid?"

He told them about meeting a woman who had soup.

Una's eyes lit up. "Vita!"

"I don't know her name, but she gave me what she called 'the soup of life.' After I drank it, I felt better than I had in years. So I came to join you. It was only when I got outside of the city that I began feeling tired."

"Can you walk?" Julien asked his father.

"Yes, if you'll help me."

They set their sight on the city in the distance and walked slowly, Julien on one side of Baba, and Una on the other.

One look at Baba's face told Una that all this talking had used up too much of his energy, so Una began to talk—to babble, really—to give Baba a chance to rest and to draw attention away from their worries. "Julien told me that you are a botanical collector. I used to have a wonderful scent collection. I had rose and frankincense, cassia and clove, bergamot and sandalwood. Calendula, peppermint, anise, and hibiscus . . ."

Baba listened, interrupting her only with bouts of coughing. The rotting scent from his lungs grew worse with each cough. Una looked at Julien, uncertain if he could tell what was wrong.

"What happened to it?" Baba asked.

Maybe it was from the lack of sleep, but Una began to giggle. "It was eaten by a wild sow and her five piglets."

Baba raised his eyebrows.

"The only thing left was oil of hartshorn."

At that, Baba let out a burst of laughter. "And no wonder. Did you have spikenard, too?"

"Oh yes. I forgot that one."

Baba pursed his lips, thinking. "Almond?"

"Yes, I had almond and pistachio, as well."

"Balm of Gilead?"

Una furrowed her brows. "I don't know that one."

"That's rockrose," Julien said. "We never did get to that, but perhaps we can find it another time."

His words triggered the memory of the previous night's adventure. "Julien! I forgot! Did you tell your father what we found?" Una exclaimed.

"Angel's wings?" Baba said, his face lit with hope.

Julien's eyes brightened and a wide smile filled his whole face. "We found angel's wings, but they weren't the right scent. So instead, we found something better."

Baba grabbed Julien's arm. "The silva? Did you find the silva?"

Una nodded. "That's why we're covered in mud!" Una related the experience—seeing the foxfire, getting stuck in the bog, getting unstuck, and then building a bridge to the silva flower.

Even with this happy news, they soon slowed to the point where Baba was barely shuffling forward. His breathing was labored, and the scent of illness grew ever stronger. Una tried to catch Julien's eye, but his focus was entirely on his father. So she stopped, causing the other two to stop with her.

"Sir? I think you must rest."

She finally caught Julien's eye; his glance sent waves of gratitude her way.

Baba nodded. "I am sorry I am so slow."

"I am not worried about our speed, but your health."

He patted her arm. "Yes, I will rest, then."

They guided Baba toward a large stone near their path and helped him sit. His breath came out in wheezes, and he began to cough.

And cough.

And cough some more.

56

Una and Julien

Una exchanged a look with Julien. "I'll go find some shelter," she said. "I don't think we'll make it home today."

Julien nodded, then sat down next to his father.

Baba breathed raggedly between coughing spells. "I'm sorry, son."

Julien listened to the frayed sound of his father's heartbeat. *Hurry, hurry, hurry,* he thought, mentally urging Una on.

Though it seemed like an eternity, it was only a few minutes before Una was back. "There's a little cave around the next bend, near the waterfall."

Una and Julien each took one side and helped Baba to the place Una had found. They laid him down gently, and he began shivering uncontrollably in the chilly morning air. Una wished Ovid was with them. He would know what to do. Una didn't, for she had never seen sickness like this.

Julien had, though—just never quite this bad. "Do you know what horehound looks like?"

Una shook her head, so Julien picked up a small stone and drew in the dirt at his feet. "It's bushy and has ruffly leaves like this. And there are flowers between the leaves and square stems. Can you look for some? Bring back as much as you can."

Una nodded and took off, her gaze sweeping the area for the plant.

Meanwhile, Julien sat by Baba and held his hand.

"Una . . . ," Baba began, but his words were taken by coughing.

"Una's looking for horehound. You'll be better soon."

Baba nodded, gripped Julien's hand tightly, and closed his eyes.

Hurry, Julien thought once more, wishing he could call Una back with whatever horehound she had collected.

Baba's breathing became shallow.

By the time Una returned clutching a fistful of horehound stems, Baba was sleeping. Julien had built a small fire and was heating a pot of water. He took the horehound and stripped the leaves and flowers off, then ripped them into pieces and put them in the water to steep.

Una stood off to the side. "I hope that's enough." When Julien didn't respond, she said, "I can go look for more if you'd like?"

"No. This is enough for now." It wasn't really enough, but

Julien didn't want Una to leave again. He didn't want to be alone with his fear.

Julien returned to Baba's side, holding his hand. Baba's heartbeat had been the most centering sound for Julien throughout his life. When Julien had been little and woke in the night, he listened for the sound of Baba's heartbeat to calm him. Its music gave him courage. But now, its music struggled through his wheezing breaths.

Baba's eyes flickered. Julien patted his hand and said, "I have some tea for you to drink. It'll help."

He motioned for Una to bring the pot sitting at the edge of the fire. She carried it to him, and watched as Julien used a cupped leaf to spoon tea into Baba's mouth. Baba swallowed a few drops, then closed his eyes once more and slept.

"You should rest, too," Una said, yawning.

Julien nodded—he knew Una was right—but he didn't think he'd be able to fall asleep. No doubt, he'd be tired later, but right now, there was too much worry in his heart. Julien closed his eyes anyway, and sure enough, soon his breathing steadied, his muscles relaxed, and he became lost in a very deep sleep.

Una tried to stay awake tending the fire. But their struggles in the bog and the late-night hike had been strenuous, and she, too, fell asleep. The fire went out.

58

Una

have to spend the whole day combing the moun-
king for Baba, because her friend the wind gave her
h in the right direction. But more importantly, the
d the scent of her soup.

elled the soup before she saw Vita. She followed it,
 see the old woman and her cart of soup trundling
rly undetectable path.

Ve need more soup!"

pped her cart, pulled out a ladle and bowl, and
d to the soup pot. "Yes, my dear. Yesterday's batch
 an important ingredient, and I've been looking for
nan since daybreak to give him more."

Baba!"

ow this sick man?" At Una's response, Vita quickly
 bowl and handed it to the girl. "Take this and go.

57

Everyone

At the same time Julien discovered his father, the guards
from the Magister Populi arose. Vita was long gone, and so was
her soup. The captain of the guard was quite certain Vita knew
more than she let on, so he sent word to the Magister Populi
and followed the tracks left by the soup cart.

Meanwhile, Cassius had run into his brothers again after
having escaped the hornets with about a dozen unfortunately
placed stings. After a weak reprimand, his brothers let him join
them again, with only the Weasel objecting. They held out
hope that they would still be able to find Una and collect ransom for her. They thought Una could not have gone far, but as
is often the case when grown men judge the abilities of girls,
they grossly underestimated her.

And lastly, there was a very sore and very dirty Florian, still seeking the silva flower and the girl, hoping to be able to pay back his debt to Brutus.

This was the population roving in the wilderness that day when Julien woke for the second time that morning. He immediately went to Baba. Baba still slept, his breathing shallow and tight, his heartbeat almost timid. Julien wished there was something he could say to Baba—something about hope, about persistence—but there was nothing he could say that would make Baba well again.

Una awoke, stiff from their long hike and bruised from sleeping in an awkward position. She turned to Julien, who held Baba's hand. "Is he any better?"

Julien looked up, the skin around his eyes dark and weary. "No change."

Una stood. "I'll go look for more horehound."

But Una found no horehound. She was certain that she had picked clean the only patch of it for miles around. As she searched, she thought if she could find Vita, she might be able to get some more of the soup to help Baba, which might actually be better than the horehound tea.

That was unlikely as Una had no idea where Vita might be or even where she was herself. She also didn't know where Cassius could be, although she was confident that he was still looking for her. So Una kept her head down, scouring the ground for any sight of horehound, and hoping against hope that she'd get lucky and come across something that might help Julien's father.

Instead of finding someth
prints from a group of men. T
as if the owners walked in a d
men she knew who walked lik
the Regiment of the Magister
sent them to look for her, but sh
bring her home, ignoring her pl
So she tread even more careful

Vita, for her part, attempt
day before to make amends fo
life-giving, but she was having
men and women are often crea
step in the same river twice, for
one was where they had been
man who had been so sick. Of
find, he was the one she worrie

If the sick man wasn't whe
him where he was—even if she
the entire mountainside.

Vita didn
tainside l
a gentle p
wind carr

Una s
overjoyed
along a n

"Vita!
Vita
lifted the
was missi
a very sic
"Tha
"You
dished ou

I'll follow along behind. You look like you could use some soup yourself."

"Thank you, Vita!"

But before she could go, a man stepped out from behind a tree.

Cassius.

Another appeared. Then another.

Una did not stop to think. She took off running through the trees to where Julien and his father waited.

Cassius and his men followed.

Vita did not like the looks of these men. As she watched the girl's retreating form, Vita wondered if she had done the right thing by remaining silent when the guards asked her if she had seen a girl. While it was true that she had cared for her eight younger siblings at Una's age, it was also true that she didn't have a choice in those responsibilities. This girl did. She carried too much burden on her shoulders, and it seemed to Vita that she didn't have to bear all of this on her own.

She would call for those guards, and let the wind bring them to her. She would give them soup, because this soup was life-giving soup after all. And it looked like they would soon have a challenge on their hands. As she followed behind Una, she recited, "Soup of life has spice and lime, chiles, garlic, luck, and time." She let the wind carry her voice and the scent of her soup away, all the while hoping for luck, because she sensed there wasn't much time.

When Una had left the small cave, Julien sat next to Baba.

He watched his chest rise in shallow breaths. He studied his face, pale and gray instead of rosy and spirited, the way it used to be.

Julien wanted to take Baba's hand, to hold it in his own, but he was afraid that if he did, he would wake Baba and he knew Baba needed to sleep.

So he sat there studying his breath, listening to the faint cadence of his heartbeat.

"Please don't go, Baba," he whispered. "Please don't. I couldn't bear it if you left me."

Julien felt the sting of tears and quickly dug his fists into his eyes to halt the flow of emotion.

As he watched Baba's quiet sleep, words bubbled up and poured out of him. "Baba, I have to tell you something. I can't smell. I don't even know what smell is. I won't ever become a gifted gatherer like you."

With those words spoken aloud, Julien knew they were true. He knew he would never be like his father. Something in him was broken, and he had no way to fix it.

Baba's weak voice cut into Julien's misery. "My son . . ."

Julien reached for his father's hand.

"You will not be a gatherer like me," Baba said slowly and with great effort.

The tears came then. His beloved father knew he was not good enough.

But Baba continued, "Because you will become greater than I ever was. You have a gift for finding all the best that the world offers." The words taxed Baba, and he coughed until his chest rattled.

Julien helped Baba to sit up so he could breathe more easily. When the coughing stopped, Baba spoke again. "You see the best in everything. Trust that gift."

Julien gently settled Baba back against the rock and took his hand again, his tears flowing freely. "I love you, Baba."

"You are the greatest joy in my life," Baba whispered, and closed his eyes. "How I love you."

59

Una and Julien

Una ran as if her life depended on it, for it very well might have—both hers and Baba's. She could guess what Cassius wanted, since he was still with the marauders. It was not what she wanted. What she wanted was to save Julien's father, and the only way that would happen was if she got him the soup. Footfall after footfall, Una tried to not let any of the soup slop over the edge of the bowl, for she didn't want to waste a single drop. No matter how careful she was, though, much of the soup spilled onto her hand and down her arm.

She dodged tree, boulder, bush, and stream, running as fast as she could. She could almost feel her mother alongside her. She wished that were so, because then she could ask her what to do, how to move forward in a life where she felt stuck. But her mother wasn't there. Una would have to figure out what to do on her own.

Right now, all she knew was that she had to get the soup to Julien and still get away from both Uncle Cassius *and* her father's guards. But she couldn't outrun all of them. She had to make a choice.

Get the soup to Julien and get caught.

Or ditch the soup and escape.

Neither was a good option. But Julien was her friend, and she knew what it was like to lose a parent.

She would bring the soup to Julien and try not to get caught. Perhaps the cave would hide them—at least for a while.

She dodged a tree and crouched behind some bushes. Miraculously, Cassius and the marauders chasing her ran by. When they were far enough away, she hurried back around to the shelter.

"Julien," she whispered. "I couldn't find more horehound, but I have something better. I have soup!"

Julien was sitting at his father's side, holding his hand. He gently placed Baba's hand on his chest and turned to Una with a grief-stricken face.

Una held out the bowl. "Wake him up, if you must. I know it will help."

Julien didn't take the bowl of soup.

"It's better than the horehound tea. It will work," she insisted. But she could smell death just as she could smell life. The only scent of life came from Julien. "The soup . . . ," Una said quietly, shaking her head. "No."

Julien looked lost. He felt lost, too. All of Baba's sounds

that had accompanied him throughout his lifetime had been silenced. There was nothing but a void, a hush, a stillness, as if all the life and light in the world had been extinguished. Una spoke to him, but he could not hear her. He couldn't even cry, his grief was so great. Crying would make noise and noise would mean he was alive. Alive in a world without Baba, utterly alone. So he remained silent, all the grief and anguish and fear bottled inside him.

60

Una and Julien

Julien stood and carried the sack containing the silva flower out of the cave. Una followed, still holding the soup. The hollow silence of the cave haunted him. It taunted him. Julien set the sack down, then went to the largest rock near the mouth of the cave. He tried to push it, but the stone was sunken into the ground. It was far too heavy to move on his own, but he tried anyway, again and again, pushing it, shoving it, beating on it with his hands. When it didn't move the slightest bit, he sank down and wept with his back turned to Una.

Una felt his grief. It mirrored her own, though Julien's was fresh, while hers had been a constant companion for years. She let herself weep along with him. His loss was hers, just as her loss was his.

An idea came to Una as she cried. Slowly, she wiped her eyes and set down the bowl of soup. She opened her pack to find the oil of hartshorn—the one scent from her collection that always gave her courage. They needed courage now, both of them.

"This is the best thing I can give you right now," she told Julien. She took off the cap and waved the vial under Julien's nose.

He looked baffled as a ticklish sensation crawled through his nose and belly-flopped into his gut. He smelled nothing, but he heard an intensity rushing out of the vial that made him want to cry even more.

Una took a whiff, too, before closing the bottle. Bitterness and despair were followed quickly by an exhilarating courage. She saw the change in Julien's face, too. He might not be able to smell, but he could feel the power of the hartshorn. It took over, wrapping them both in strength. She put the bottle away.

Julien took a deep breath. His eyes looked clearer.

Una said, "Something about that scent leaves me with courage. Even if you couldn't smell it, I had hoped it would give you the same feeling. I don't have much to offer besides my friendship, but I can give you a small bit of courage."

"Thank you." Julien looked back at the cave. "He was happy out here."

"I think he was happiest when he was with you," Una said.

They sat in quiet for some time before Julien said, "I thought Baba would be able to help you find the right scent."

Una looked away. "I don't think my mother's scent can be found." The possibility of archangels had darted around her in the past few days, as if a host of heavenly beings gathered just out of reach, brushing past her with feathery wings but never descending low enough for her to grasp. The scent of her mother was gone, and there was nothing she could do about it.

The two sat there, trying to be brave, trying to have courage, but the weight of their loss was heavy to bear.

61

Una, Julien, and Vita

The sound of the soup cart approached them along with the scent of hot tang.

Vita trundled into the clearing by the cave. She looked from one child to the other and then back again.

"Oh, my dears," she said, holding her arms out to both of them. Though Julien had never officially met Vita, her offer of comfort was too great, and they both flew into her arms where the three of them cried together, holding each other tightly. "I'm so, so sorry. My soup wasn't right when I gave it to your father. It should have been right. This is all my fault."

"He'd been sick for years," Julien said through his tears. "I don't think your soup could have saved him."

Vita wiped her face with a brightly colored handkerchief. "He won't suffer any more, but that doesn't make it any easier for you." She squeezed Julien's shoulder, then folded her handkerchief and put it away. "You both need some soup," she said. "Soup will help."

Una and Julien obediently drank a bowl of her fiery broth, because neither had the heart to refuse her. Surprisingly, it did help. When they finished and returned the bowls, Vita asked, "What will you do now?"

Julien looked away, very much uncertain about his future. He could go back to his home, but he hadn't been endorsed by the other collectors yet, so he wouldn't be allowed to sell to the makers in the market. He didn't have Baba's knowledge about negotiating, anyway. Julien wasn't sure where his daily meals were going to come from.

As if reading his mind, Vita said, "My soup pot will always be full for you. You too, dear girl, but I suspect there's someone with a much more elegant soup pot waiting for you."

For the first time since leaving home, Una felt guilty and wondered if her father *had* noted her absence. Would he be worried? Ovid surely knew that she was gone; he had sent supplies with Julien. But unless Ovid had told him, her father knew nothing. She flushed. "How did you know?"

"I came across someone looking for you."

Startled, Una looked at Julien. "Cassius?"

"Yes?" a voice called from above the waterfall.

And there he was once again, along with the other marauders. Una, Julien, and Vita were surrounded.

Under different circumstances, Una would have run. She would have run as fast as an archangel's wings could beat.

She would have vanished like a scent blown by a whirlwind. But Julien's father was dead, and Julien needed her. So Una stayed put.

Julien was still so wrapped up in his grief that it didn't even occur to him to run.

Vita took one look at the marauders and knew deep in her very old bones that these were men to avoid. But she, herself, was too old to run, and she was not going to leave these children at their mercy. The only weapon she had was her soup.

"Would you like some soup?" she asked with a slight waver to her voice. "It's life-giving soup. Soup of life has spice and lime, chiles, garlic, luck, and time."

Cassius snorted.

Vita knew he wouldn't want her soup, but she needed a simple distraction.

It didn't work.

Cassius jumped down to them. "You should not have left," he told Una. "I have spent a great deal of time looking for you. What would my mother and father think if they knew you had rejected my invitation and their hospitality?"

Una said nothing, for what could she say? That she no longer trusted Cassius? That his brothers frightened her? That she knew she was simply a pawn to them?

Cassius began walking toward her, and his scent—now threatening—preceded him.

It was only then that Una truly recognized the danger she was in—the danger all three of them were in. For she had put Julien and Vita in harm's way, too.

Cassius look another step toward her. "So what shall we do? Will you come with us now? And your young friend there—he can go look for the silva flower."

"We already found the silva flower," Una said, pointing to the sack lying forgotten behind them.

But the sack wasn't entirely forgotten, for someone else was pawing through it—someone who had once been clean and fine smelling with expensive clothes, but who now was filthy, smelly, and swollen by hornet stings.

Florian gave a squeak and backed away from the sack, looking from Cassius to Brutus and then to Una. Una didn't even try to stop him.

"I know you want money from the Magister Populi in exchange for me," she told Cassius.

"Smart girl."

"He won't give it to you, Uncle Cassius. You got the wrong child if you expect money. I'm not a boy. He doesn't care about me."

A powerful voice came from the woods behind them. "On that point, you are wrong. I care very much."

The Magister Populi emerged from the trees, sitting astride a huge beast of a horse. He had a small army flanking him, drawn there by the trusty wind bearing the scent of Vita's soup and the telltale tracks from the cart's wheels. Their approach had been disguised by the sound of the waterfall at the edge of the cave where Baba lay.

Cassius took off running, but he had to get past Vita to

avoid the Magister Populi's men. Vita wasn't about to let him get away. She pushed the soup cart. The sturdy wheels were true, and the corner of the cart connected with Cassius, hitting him square in his side. He fell hard.

The guards restrained him, and with the other marauders surrounded, they were tied up within seconds. Even Florian couldn't escape. It was over so fast that Una didn't have time to blink.

The Magister Populi dismounted and went to Una. "My dear child, how could you think I didn't care?"

Una looked down at her feet, dried mud encrusted on her boots. Though Cassius was no longer a threat to her and she wanted to feel relief, she only felt empty. Nothing essential had changed.

Her father took a step closer to Una. "Did you really think that I didn't care?"

"You never came to see me. After Mum died. You never left your rooms."

"Oh, Una, I'm so very sorry. Your mother's death was extremely hard for me. But I should have been there for you."

Una smelled the sorrow coming off him and saw the sincerity in his face. "I wish you had."

"I wish I had, too." He opened his arms, and she fell into them and wept as if she'd never be able to stop. She cried for her lost mother, for Julien's lost father, for her lost hope, for lost time, for the great gulf of emptiness that she held within her. As she wept, she found herself breathing in her father's scent—a scent like lightning and thunder, so different from her mother's, but, maybe, almost as dear.

62

Everyone

The Magister Populi spoke, his arm still around his first child. "Let's go home now."

But Una hesitated, looking back at Julien. "Julien and Vita must come, too." And then she told him about Julien's father and Vita's soup and all that had happened that day and the previous day.

As she spoke, the Magister Populi looked at the skinny boy, his gaunt cheeks dirty and tear-stained. "I'm very sorry," he said to Julien. "I remember your father well. The first Magistrix spoke very highly of him. The gardens have never been the same since your father was head gardener. Will you consider staying with us, at the very least in your time of grief, if not longer?"

Julien looked back at the gaping cave. "I can't leave him here."

The Magister Populi lifted a hand, and one of his men hurried to his side. "Leave four of your men to give this man a proper burial."

The man nodded and signaled to three others.

"What about Vita?" Una said.

The old woman bowed before the Magister Populi and said, "I would offer you soup, sir, if I could." She looked helplessly at the ground where the contents of her soup pot had spilled, sacrificed to capture Cassius.

"Would you join us, too, Grandmother? I should very much like to taste your soup."

Vita was pleased beyond words.

But before they could go anywhere, Una reached into the sack that Florian had dropped when he was surrounded by the soldiers. She pulled out a slightly wilted but still sturdy plant with vivid green leaves and a single large bud. "I have the silva flower for you." She held it out to her father.

Baffled, he said, "I don't understand. That was going to be my gift to you."

"I know. Ovid told me. I wanted to find it so I could prove to you that I was capable of doing something on my own, that I was worth your time."

The Magister Populi looked stricken.

Una stared at her feet. "The last time I saw you, you left without even looking at me. Your new son was more important than me because I'm not a boy, and I'll never be the next Magister."

"No," he said. "The law forbids you from being a Magister."

Una felt frustration growing inside her at this arbitrary law and her luck at being born a girl.

"But that doesn't mean you can't be a Magistrix."

Una's mouth dropped open.

"You have shown more compassion, more bravery, and more level-headedness than men five times your age. I think a change in the way we do things is in order."

At a nod from the Magister Populi, the guards helped Una, Julien, and Vita onto horses and the group returned to the city, the Magister Populi leading the way.

Ruana, Una's paste-scented stepmother, met them at the gate. The anxious look on her face disappeared when she spotted them. Ruana still seemed like an exotic bird to Una, but clearly her feathers had been ruffled by Una's absence.

She ran out to meet them. Ruana pulled Una down from her horse and wrapped her in an embrace. And Una noticed a strange thing: her stepmother's paste scent wasn't so strong. Now the woman smelled almost sweet, as if her paste had been used to hold everything together.

Ovid was there to greet them, too. His gaze took in Baba's absence, but he only said, "You both look as if you could use some care. Come, let me tend to you."

63

Julien

Julien soaked in the same tub that his father had soaked in days earlier. The warm water was a balm to his tired body, but it did nothing for his aching heart. He kept thinking *if only*. If only Florian hadn't taken Baba to jail. If only he hadn't left Baba at the Official Residence. If only Vita had given Baba the right soup. If only the angel's wings had been the right scent. If only he and Una hadn't gotten stuck on the bog that night. If only Cassius had been a good person.

But then, he realized that if all of these *if only*s hadn't happened, he would never have met Una, his first real friend. He would never have met Ovid or Vita. He would never have known that his abilities were as special as Baba's had been, for it was the combination of his unique abilities with Una's that allowed them to find the silva flower. He would never have realized his own capabilities.

Julien also knew there was one more big *if only*: if only Baba hadn't left the Official Residence. If only he had stayed. If only he had rested. If only he had let Ovid take care of him.

But he didn't.

And that was his choice. There was nothing Julien could have done about that. Baba left because he wanted to be with Julien and Una. He wanted to be out looking for the late Magistrix's favorite flowers.

Julien took a deep breath and submerged himself in the water. He missed Baba. He missed him more than he could express, and he knew he would miss him always. But he also knew that he would be all right. He rose from the water, certain that Baba would be glad that he was in the Official Residence, that he would be taking on the care of the gardens that Baba had once tended. Baba would be delighted that Julien could bring his skills, special as they were, to the world around him. Instead of smelling the flowers and the plants like Baba, he would hear them. He would listen to them, and let them grow and flourish in the way that they needed, just as he would grow and flourish in the way he needed.

And Baba would be glad that he had a true friend: Una.

He stepped out of the tub and dried off, then dressed in the new clothes that Ovid had given him, ready to step into his new life at the Official Residence.

64

Una

Back in the courtyard garden, next to the window with the showy white blossoms—the angel's wings—Una's thoughts were drawn to the events of the past week and how she had stood in that very spot when she first learned that her mother had a younger brother, whom she had loved and cared for. She wondered if things would have turned out differently if Cassius had said goodbye to her mother before she left to marry the Magister Populi. Maybe he would have carried a portion of her love inside of him and maybe that would have influenced Cassius to choose a more honest path than he had. For he had become a scoundrel, and was being held in prison awaiting trial. She didn't know what would become of Cassius and the rest of the marauders, some of whom were likely more of her uncles. She didn't know if her father would ever tell her about the history between their two families. She didn't know if there would be future trouble because of this imprisonment.

But she did know that like her mother, she had a younger brother. In fact, she had two. And she wasn't about to let history repeat itself. No longer would she be on her own, just Una. With her younger brother, she'd be part of a duo. And with Ruana's son, they'd be a tribe.

She was still somewhat startled by Ruana's relief at her return, surprised by her embrace, stunned at her affection. In fact, Ruana reacted much like her own mother would have. The thought warmed her, and she found that she felt differently about Ruana now. Maybe there was more to Ruana than the scent of paste. Maybe she needed Ruana as much as her father did.

Indeed, her relationship with her father would be different, too. He had said that her lessons would shift to include more history and more geography, and would also include law and economics, in preparation for her to assume a greater role in governing their nation. Her days would be filled in a way they hadn't been before, but Una looked forward to the challenge, because it gave her new purpose. Being Magistrix would be a heavy responsibility, but Una felt deep inside that she had been born to this role—by both birth and experience—and she was grateful to have a chance to make a real impact on the future of their land.

And then there was Julien. Una smiled when she thought of him. What luck had brought her to meet him! What luck to have a friend who knew her for who she was, and not just as the First Daughter or the future Magistrix. She could trust him, and that was a real gift. Yes, he was acting as head gardener for now, but Una suspected he might have a future in diplomacy if he wanted. And regardless, she would make sure he had all the cucumbers he ever desired.

Into her thoughts charged a five-year-old boy with crazy hair. "Una! What are we going to play today?" Una nearly fell over from the force of his small body hugging her. She wrapped her arms around him and spun him in a circle, lifting his feet off the ground until he laughed and laughed, deliriously happy at the attention from his older sister.

When they stopped spinning, they tumbled to the ground. "I'm going to show you my garden, Theo, because before this was my garden, it was our mother's garden."

Eyes wide, the small boy said, "That sounds perfect."

Una stood and helped her younger brother to his feet. As she did so, the most curious thing happened. A scent, like the breath of an archangel, wafted through the air. She paused.

"What's wrong?" her brother asked.

"Do you smell that?"

He sniffed deeply. "Of course."

"What is it? Where is it coming from?"

"It's love, silly." And he ran off, his fingers brushing a bush that Una had shaped into a perfectly round globe—a perfect circle—with much patience.

Una followed, thinking of her mother, and how she could

remember pieces of her. She'd wished she had something to glue those pieces back together into a whole. She thought her mother's scent would do it, but Una now realized that she had been wrong. She carried all those pieces of her mother's love and memory within her, and she always would.

Acknowledgments

While luck may be a tricky, slippery thing, gratitude is rock solid. How grateful I am to be surrounded by wise, creative, and exceptional people who enrich my life and make my work infinitely better! I had the good fortune of working with Mary Kate Castellani, Cindy Loh, Allison Moore, and Annette Pollert-Morgan on the manuscript. Lucy Rose did the extraordinary cover. The rest of the Bloomsbury group continue to be a marvelous source of knowledge, good will, and hard work: Erica Barmash, Phoebe Dyer, Beth Eller, Alona Fryman, Melissa Kavonic, Jeanette Levy, Erica Loberg, Donna Mark, Jasmine Miranda, Daniel O'Connor, Oona Patrick, Valentina Rice, Teresa Sarmiento, Claire Stetzer, Chris Venkatesh. Thank you, one and all. I will always be grateful to have Michelle Witte on my side, wearing her agent hat. My writing (and my life) is much the richer for Julie Berry's brilliant contributions. The Vermont

Acknowledgments

College of Fine Arts community is truly the best writers' community. Many thanks to my Beverly Shores group, especially my pandemic writing buddies: Katie Bayerl, Rachel Hylton, Marianna Baer, Mikki Knudsen, Michael Leali, Mary Winn Heider, Varian Johnson, and Larissa Theule. Thanks also to Lydia Hall, intern extraordinaire.

Ultimately, I have written something that pays homage in a small way to the sacred relationship between parent and child. My thanks go always to my mother, Robin Woodruff, who was consistently the source of home, comfort, security, love, and brownie mixes, and to my sons, Samuel and Will, who have been a source of love, worry, pride, laughter, and oddball schemes. And where would I be without the Gingerbread Man? Much gratitude to my William, the one who will always have my heart.